"You have of a godde

Jake's husky voice sent a blush racing across Miranda's creamy skin. He smiled at the sight and reached over to stroke the rosy color at her throat. Then he crushed her to him, his hands kneading her back, her shoulders....

Miranda buried her hands in his thick, dark hair and reveled in his eager touch. She groaned, feeling the heat of his breath on her cheek.

"I want to kiss every velvety inch of you," Jake whispered. "Now, where shall I begin...?"

THE AUTHOR

Marion Smith Collins's enjoyment of
romance writing is reflected in the warmth
and gentle humor found in her books. She
and her husband, Bob, a lawyer, live in the
north Georgia mountains. "Bob has often
been the model for my heroes," admits
Marion with pride.

Marion is also proud of the close
relationship she enjoys with her children,
Katie and Rob, to whom she has dedicated
this book.

Books by Marion Smith Collins

HARLEQUIN TEMPTATION
  5–BY MUTUAL CONSENT
22–BY ANY OTHER NAME
35–THIS THING CALLED LOVE
49–ON THE SAFE SIDE

These books may be available at your local bookseller.

Don't miss any of our special offers. Write to us at the
following address for information on our newest releases.

Harlequin Reader Service
P.O. Box 52040, Phoenix, AZ 85072-2040
Canadian address: P.O. Box 2800, Postal Station A,
5170 Yonge St., Willowdale, Ont. M2N 6J3

On the Safe Side

MARION SMITH COLLINS

Harlequin Books

TORONTO • NEW YORK • LONDON
AMSTERDAM • PARIS • SYDNEY • HAMBURG
STOCKHOLM • ATHENS • TOKYO • MILAN

This book is dedicated with love to my children,
Katherine Collins Dooley and Robert Lee Collins II,
who've grown up to be my friends.

Published March 1985

ISBN 0-373-25149-1

Printed in Canada

WASHINGTON—The White House announced today the president will spend four days during the month of June at the home of Col. Donald Webster, Ret., on Sea Island, Georgia. Though the trip is being billed as a personal visit, there is speculation that the chief executive will take the opportunity to confer with his host concerning excess in Defense Department spending. Colonel Webster is the former head of the Army's Supply Corps.

1

CLOSED! Miranda Woodbarry put her hands on her hips and sighed in disgust. She glared at the door of the Sea Island Company's leasing office, and then at her watch. They must have left at five on the dot, the clock-watchers. How was she supposed to get into the beach-front cottage?

It had been a long day. Miranda was hot, tired, grumpy and very hungry. This was the last straw, she thought.

Pivoting with an impatient swing that sent her blazing red hair flying about her shoulders, she stalked back to her car and yanked the door open. Her green cotton skirt hiked well up over her bare knees as she slid across the seat, but she didn't bother to pull it down. It was cooler that way. Though summer wouldn't officially arrive for two more weeks, the heat of coastal

Georgia made her think longingly of bathing suits and shorts.

Of all days for the air-conditioning system in her four-year-old car to lose its Freon, this had to be the one. She had been driving for hours, and the crisp white blouse she had donned that morning was now limp and clinging. She tugged at its elasticized neckline. Without lowering her head she blew, her upper lip directing the stream of air to the damp crevice between her breasts.

Well, at least she was here. The thought lifted her spirits slightly. The practical thing would have been to wait until tomorrow. But Miranda wasn't feeling particularly practical, and she hadn't wanted to wait, so after dismissing her students for the final time, she had driven from the University of Georgia campus in Athens to try to reach the island resort before the office closed.

As she turned the key in the ignition, a blast of warm vented air lifted a damp thread of hair from her neck and tossed it back behind her shoulder. "Thanks a lot," she told the grilled aperture wryly. A somber voice informed her there was more fighting in Lebanon. She switched the radio off.

As she reversed from the parking space, Miranda gave a ragged sigh. The house would be locked up tight. She would have to break a window to get in, she decided, cringing at the idea. But what choice did she have?

She dismissed her guilty conscience and

swiped at the perspiration on her upper lip. Let the Sea Island Company worry about security. They'd known she was coming. If they couldn't hang around for a few minutes after closing time.... She glanced at her watch again. Slightly more than a few minutes, she admitted ruefully as she turned back onto the main road.

Three blocks farther she made a sharp right. At the end of the short street the ocean beckoned. She would have liked nothing better than to stop right there, pull off her shoes and sink her toes into the soft white sand. Inhaling the mind-clearing scent of salt air, she would have let the soothing sound of the surf ease the tension from her shoulders.

She resisted the lure, steering the car between two stucco pillars into the courtyard of cottage #96 as she ticked off her priorities—get into the house, have a shower and find something to eat.

The last would necessitate a trip either to the market or to one of the many restaurants on St. Simon's Island. A restaurant was quickly vetoed as was the thought of dining in splendor at the more formal hotel only three blocks away. Tonight a sandwich on the beach held more appeal.

For a long moment she sat looking at the house. Built in the style of a French country manor, it was as badly misnamed as the rest of the homes on Sea Island. Cottages, indeed!

Five minutes later she stood with her hands on her hips, her green eyes raking the vine-

streaked house almost accusingly. Breaking in
upstairs was out of the question. And she
would hate to destroy the French doors or Pal-
ladian windows that faced the ocean, so she
supposed it would have to be the kitchen. She
had already searched the garage and the pool
house. Nothing, not a hoe, not a shovel, not
even a beach umbrella had been left out.

Miranda went back to the car and reached inside for her purse. Hefting its weight a few
times she decided it would have to do. She approached the window, gingerly avoiding the
spiky shrubbery, and stood tiptoe to peer inside. Copper pans, hanging neatly from their
rack, winked at her in the late afternoon sunlight.

She took a deep breath and stepped back.
Holding the heavy canvas bag by its serviceable
strap, she swung it with all her might.

There was a loud, satisfying crash, and she
heard the glass scatter inside the house. "Done,"
she muttered. A rush of cool air fanned her face.
At least the company had turned on the air-
conditioning. Now if she could just get inside to
enjoy it . . . .

Carefully she loosened the remaining shards
from the window frame and tossed them aside.
Slinging the big bag over the sill she let it
drop. Then with both hands she hoisted herself
up.

The window was small and there was no way
to turn, so she wiggled in head first. With arms
straight and stiff, and hands gripping the sill,

she hesitated until she felt securely balanced. When she was sure that she wasn't going to do a nose dive into the sink, she carefully inched one hand free from under her stomach to grasp the side of the window. If she could get one foot up to the sill . . . .

Miranda had no warning. Suddenly her thighs were grabbed from behind. She threw back her head in stunned amazement, bumping it painfully on the window frame. A shower of stars crossed her vision. Her fingers slipped grasping for purchase, and the fleshy part of her palm caught on a sharp piece of glass.

"Ouch! Dammit!" she yelled.

At the same moment a deep masculine voice said, "Oh, no you don't!"

Strong hands pulled her unceremoniously back through the window and deposited her firmly on the ground. She stumbled and would have sat on the sharp spikes of a palmetto had the stranger not kept a steadfast grip on her arm.

She was far beyond being grateful. "Who the hell are you?" She glared up, and farther up, into the blackest eyes she'd ever seen. But their color was wasted on her. All she saw was the man's hard, glacial expression. His jaw was firm and unyielding, producing within her a shiver of apprehension she tried to dismiss. After all, *she* was where she was supposed to be.

"Who the hell are *you*?" he returned coldly, awaiting her explanation as though it was his due. He ignored her glower.

Perversely, the stranger's control immediately dissolved Miranda's misgivings and fueled her anger to a flash point. This stupid man had caused her to bump her head and cut her hand, and he stood there looking down at her as though she were an intrusion he could do without.

Miranda didn't even think to be frightened as she struggled for freedom again, until she realized three things: that the man was very strong, that his jaw was now clenched in stiff-necked determination and that he had no intention of releasing her arm. Suddenly it was an all out fight.

She spun toward him rather than away, catching him momentarily by surprise. Her nails raked his face while her foot came up to connect with a jean-clad shin, unfortunately falling short of its original target. "Let go of me, you bastard!" she puffed furiously.

The man jerked his head back out of the range of her nails. "Calm down, sister," he growled. "You'd better have a good explanation." He held her easily at arm's length, nullifying her second attempt to do damage to a vulnerable portion of his anatomy. Again he was completely in command—of her and of himself.

Which was more than she could say. Miranda ground her teeth with frustration, feeling helpless at her obvious physical limitations. She couldn't fight him, and that made her madder than ever. She was panting with exertion, and her arm throbbed from his grip. This was a ridiculous situation.

"Now, would you like to explain?" he asked fiercely. "Breaking and entering...with felonious intent." His fingers casually touched his cheek and came away with a smear of blood. If possible his expression became more impassive. "Assault. Destroying private property while performing a seditious act."

"Seditious? That's treason. You're crazy!"

A muscle in his tanned throat jumped, she noticed with satisfaction. He didn't like being called crazy. But otherwise he remained unmoved.

Belatedly it dawned on Miranda that his intention wasn't really to hurt her. His long, lean body was like that of a panther, all power and raw assurance, but the strength was leashed, well under control, although his hands were so strong that the circulation in her arm was being cut off.

Her mother's favorite Southern belle homily came back to her: more flies are caught with honey than with vinegar. She faced the fact that she'd get further with this man using her mind rather than her emotions. With blood dripping from one hand, and the other holding her aching head, she took a breath to calm her temper. The time had come for rational thinking.

The man wasn't a Sea Island security guard. They all wore uniforms, and he was dressed casually in jeans and a knit shirt. He must be a workman of some kind. But even if he had misunderstood her reason for climbing in through the window, he had no right to grab her in such an undignified way.

She bit back her next hostile thought. *Honey*, she reminded herself. She moistened her lips. "There's been a terrible mistake," she told him, her accent almost dripping the stuff, and looked up at him with what she hoped was a limpid gaze. Then her lashes fell, fluttering beguilingly as Scarlett's had done.

The first genuinely emotional response she'd had from him was not at all what she'd expected. His laugh was sharp and threatening. "Sorry, honey," he snarled.

Her eyes popped open. Honey? Had he read her mind? The Southern charm hadn't worked. Not only had it not worked, it had backfired with a vengeance.

His features twisted in contempt at her efforts. It was a breach in the implacable mask he'd worn, but Miranda was beyond appreciating it. She was almost in sympathy with him, appalled at herself for trying such tactics.

"I'm not open for that kind of explanation." The compelling dark eyes surveyed her with insulting thoroughness from her shoes to the wild and slightly damp mane of red hair. His brows came together in a scowl. "The package is attractive but I think I can manage to resist," he informed her sarcastically. His grip tightened and he gave her a rough shake, deliberately meant to be intimidating. "Lady, you are in trouble!"

The workman, or whatever he was, didn't

know Miranda. She was not easily intimidated, even by a man whose shoulders would have rivaled an Olympic discus thrower's. Fueled by chagrin at her own foolishness, her dampened anger reignited immediately at his words. The rough shaking magnified it tenfold and filled her with a white-hot fury.

She drew in a deep, body-straightening breath and squared her shoulders. This *was* the last straw! Any person who would dare to speak to Miranda Woodbarry and handle her in such a manner deserved a tongue-lashing he wouldn't soon forget. A primitive need to best an opponent welled up within her. Her indignation grew swiftly into a rare rage, and Miranda's redheaded rage was something to see. She might not be up to his weight physically, but with her training in theater, she could verbally damn a man to within an inch of his life.

Her clear green eyes narrowed, turned a yellow-apple color and shot burning golden arrows into the hard ice of his. Her chin lifted, her jaw clenched, sculpting the planes of high cheekbones in sharp relief, giving her the look of a medieval sorcerer about to invoke the spirits of the Dark Ages. A vein in her temple throbbed, threatening to burst. She spoke through her teeth, her voice dangerous and menacingly low as she delivered her words like a load of buckshot.

"You fool! What the hell do you think you're doing shaking me like that? I'll see you hanged on Sunday, you buzzard! I'll have you cow-kicked and hornswoggled if you don't let go of me this second, you son of an outcast skunk!" She ranted on, calling upon every curse from the fifth century to the twentieth that her churning brain could dredge up, profaning him for at least a thousand years after his death.

She would put the fear of God into this overgrown lump of earth, she vowed. "I'll have you exiled so far that the lower depths of Hades will seem like heaven! Your children will be polywogs and cankerworms!"

The man was obviously, maddeningly unimpressed. He listened to her tirade with a bored expression, as though he had heard it all before, and he didn't loosen his grip.

That wooden mien of indifference made Miranda even more furious. "You great clumsy hulk! You spark for the fireside of Lucifer! You . . . you . . . ." She sputtered, running out of epithets as she ran out of breath, then inhaled long and deep, ready to begin again.

Suddenly she swallowed and choked. Her jaw went slack and her eyes grew unbelievably large in a face drained of color. Two men in dark suits had come running around the corner of the house with guns drawn. Pointed into the air . . . but definitely guns, and definitely drawn!

Miranda gulped. Her eyes flew from the two men to the one who still held her and back again. Guns. Good God, they had guns!

"Need any help, Jake?" one of the armed men asked seriously. He was talking to her captor.

The second man spoke grimly. "I'm glad The

Man isn't here yet. He wouldn't have been pleased. You could hear her squawking from a mile away."

"I think I can handle her," the man they called Jake answered. The words were delivered in a quick, terse, no-nonsense tone. "But hang around for a minute. She's a hotheaded little bitch."

Without thinking, Miranda started to protest. "I'm not a—" But all at once she was spun around and pushed to face the wall of the house. Instinctively she lifted her forearms to catch herself.

She was too confused at first to realize what was happening as the man's hands moved across her shoulders and down her sides. But when they circled her body to run thoroughly, if dispassionately, over her breasts and stomach, the shock that had gripped her at the unexpected sight of the other men dissolved. She gasped. "What on earth ... ?"

"Shut up," Jake ground out as his hands swept under her skirt, carefully patting each leg all the way up to where her thighs joined.

It was as though she were actually being violated. The sudden realization that this stranger had total disregard for her person left her feeling abused, assaulted, almost raped by the heartless touch. Her shield of anger was no protection against the feather of dread that traced down her spine. Who *were* these people? What was happening to her? "Please," she implored, starting to turn.

She was roughly shoved against the house again, scraping her nose on the abrasive stucco. A huge palm flattened between her shoulder blades, holding her there.

It was too much even for a strong person to endure, she told herself. A long drive after the many long days and late nights that defined the end of the school year, the lack of anything to eat since breakfast, the loneliness of arriving at an empty house, the frustrating experience of not being able to get inside by any conventional means and now this callous abuse—it was just too much. She laid her cheek on the sun-warmed wall of the house and began to cry.

Miranda rarely cried, and when she did it was not a pretty sight. Her large emerald eyes dulled to a shade of grayish verdigris, like the weedy flotsam tossed up from the bottom of a stormy sea. She didn't cry in tiny ladylike sobs, but noisily, with great convulsive swallows. And the tears didn't roll down her cheeks like sweet-salty drops; instead they poured, wetting the lower half of her face with the thoroughness of a water hose. She squeezed her eyes shut in an unsuccessful attempt to stop the flow.

"P-please," she wailed. "I don't know why you're here but please, leave me alone. If you're burglars take what you want and go. There isn't any jewelry or money—my parents are away for the summer—but there are a couple of television sets, and . . . and I'll write you a check if you like." She snuffled loudly. "But please, just . . . just go."

All at once the hand against her back was jerked away as if it had been burned. There was dead silence behind her.

The three men looked at each other and then lifted their eyes heavenward as if seeking deliverance. Soundlessly the one they called Jake ran a hand around the back of his neck and waved the other two away. They went gratefully, with sympathetic grins, replacing the revolvers in shoulder holsters beneath their jackets.

Jake Stewart tried to thrust his hands into the back pockets of the jeans he'd pulled on hastily when he'd first heard the sound of the car. He had to work his fingers back and forth a bit to ease the shrunken denim fabric, just back from the laundry. It gave him something to do while he stared down at the miserable form huddled against the wall and wondered what the hell she was doing breaking into her own house.

She was the daughter, of course. Miranda Woodbarry.

For a minute he was furious with her for putting him in this position. What was he supposed to think? The woman attacked like a thirty-year marine bucking for sergeant, and cursed like a drunk sailor on weekend leave. He worked one hand out of his back pocket and raked his fingers through his dark hair. Then he tugged at the thick, wiry strands. Dammit!

Without being told, his computer memory searched its files for the pertinent facts about Miranda Woodbarry, sketchy though they were. Twenty-eight years old; divorced from one

‐harles Springer; had taken back her maiden name. She was presently living in Athens, an instructor at the University of Georgia; only child of Peter Adams Woodbarry and Mary Louise Fitzgerald Woodbarry, who were formerly of Macon, Georgia, where Peter had been in the insurance business. Now the parents were permanent residents of Sea Island, and were traveling in Europe for the summer. There was no record of any kind against them.

The facts raced across the screen of Jake's mind on one level, while on another he tried to decide how to handle the situation. Break-ins and crime on the island were rare but not unknown. He had jumped to a logical conclusion, he told himself. In his job there was no time for polite inquiry. You had to act first and ask questions later, and if one erred on the side of over-vigilance, then so much the better. Most people appreciated this. He just hoped that the fiery redhead was one of those people. Otherwise he was in for a month of explanations and a mountain of forms to be filled out, justifying his actions.

"Miss Woodbarry?" he said quietly. But she didn't seem to hear him. Or maybe she was ignoring him deliberately. Damn. The way she cried — with all the abandon of a toddler — made him feel like an animal.

His teeth worried the inside of his cheek. No, no toddler, he corrected. All woman. Not short, not tall, just a nice height. Firm, uptilted breasts that were a perfect size to fill his hands. Long smooth legs, skin like satin and a sweetly rounded bottom. Definitely not a child. His fingers curled into his palms, remembering the lush fullness of the body he had searched. He knew what she felt like with clothes on; he couldn't help wondering, even at this inappropriate moment, what she looked like without them.

Hell! What was he thinking of? He had searched women before when there was no female agent available and he'd never stopped to analyze their attributes. That was definitely unprofessional and against regulations! But he was also trained to note facts automatically, store them away in his mind for future reference.

All woman, and an extraordinary one at that. What a spectacular temper! He was surprised that lightning hadn't split the heavens to strike them both, and wondered if his children, if he ever had any, would indeed be polywogs and cankerworms. After the vehemence of her curse he wouldn't be surprised.

His customarily stern expression thawed slightly and he shrugged his wide shoulders. Now that his suspicions were alleviated he could look on the situation with a degree of humor, which would have been impossible if the man he was sworn to protect had actually been in residence.

A suspicious nature was necessary in his job, but he reluctantly admitted to a certain pleasure that he could let down his guard, for a while anyway, with this woman. Miranda Woodbarry might take some taming, but he would enjoy trying to dehorn the little devil. Tact and diplomacy were also a necessary part of his job.

With no effort at all he scooped her up, one arm across her back, one beneath her knees. His movement was lithe and smooth as he carried her to the back steps.

Miranda's eyes flew open, shimmering in real fear, and she wedged her elbows between their bodies, struggling against his superior strength. "No! Oh, no. Please!" Dear God, what was he going to do? "Please, Mr ... Jake ... please let me go."

"Sh-h-h. Nobody's going to hurt you," the stranger promised steadily, sitting down on the steps with her in his lap.

Miranda opened her mouth to scream, but he stopped the outcry before it came. Placing a finger on her lips, he spoke quickly. "I've made a mistake, Miss Woodbarry. Please don't be afraid."

Oddly, all fear faded with the gentle touch. A finger at her mouth would certainly not have stopped her scream, but something in his eyes did, something that she was unable to identify immediately. She searched the strong features. Was it regret that she saw? Self-reproach?

Nonsense, she decided. Those two emotions would be totally alien to the unyielding jaw, the firm lips, the autocratic forbearance of this man. "Don't be afraid? Of guns? Guns, for heaven's sake!" She fixed him with an accusatory glare. "Who *are* you?"

When he shifted her weight, she braced herself again, not in fear but ready to do battle.

His grasp tightened and his hand went to his back pocket, but it came away empty. "Damn," he muttered. "I don't have my wallet, but my name is Jake Stewart. I'm with the Secret Service."

Miranda wiped one eye with the back of her hand and peered at him. Was he kidding? He looked serious enough. "Secret Service? But I haven't done anything!" she protested, her tear-drenched eyes opening to their fullest.

"I'll explain. Don't cry anymore. Everything's all right. I promise you." He punctuated each short sentence with a soft pat of apology on her shoulder. In anyone else it would have been a solemn gesture, a sincere, earnest bid for forgiveness. But it was so out of character for this man that she almost smiled, until she remembered how badly she'd been used.

She had no intention of crying again. In fact she was more than surprised to find herself passive, cradled against his powerful chest, being rocked as if she were a child being comforted. She should be making another effort to put this boor in his place.

"You promise? What good is the promise of a ruffian?" she finally demanded weakly. "You're a thug." He had to be, to have subjected her to such a humiliating experience as that search. Her body burned from head to toe at the memory of his hands on her. She wiped at her face with her fingers and wriggled again, but obviously he wasn't going to let her go until he was good and ready.

He murmured soothing phrases in her ear, agreeing with both statements. "Yes. I'm a thug and a ruffian, and you would be justified in scratching my eyes out. But don't cry anymore. Damn! I've never heard a woman cry like that! Do you know how heartbroken you sound when you cry?"

His warm breath fanned wisps of hair at her temple, and Miranda wished that her heartbeat would return to something resembling its normal cadence, that the trembling in her limbs would subside. The entire episode had been a shock to her system.

He smelled like soap and woodsy cologne, she noted absently. His cheek, where it brushed her forehead, was smooth, freshly shaved.

"I know. I *look* awful, too." She gave an inelegant sniff and relaxed in his arms, not questioning why their strength seemed so reassuring all of a sudden. Or why the danger, wherever it had come from, seemed to be over. "I've never been able to cry in a pretty way." She sighed and looked up at him. "But you haven't told me what I'm supposed to have done."

The man, Jake, smiled...but slowly, very slowly, as though he was unskilled in the practice. The smile softened his dark eyes to a brown-velvet color, crinkling the corners. The furrow on one side of his face deepened, and the dark straight brows lifted. His teeth were strong and white in contrast to his tanned skin.

Miranda caught her breath. His smile was a warm, gradual surprise, like sunshine coming out over the ocean on a bleak November day. Its effect was even more potent than his physical strength.

If there was a slight hint of satisfaction in his expression, she chose to ignore it for the moment, until her curiosity was satisfied. From the cold-eyed stranger of a while ago, he had changed almost instantly into a captivating, appealing individual. How interesting, that sudden change. And how dangerous!

He was handsome and he wasn't; he was ... virile and manly. In the strong, even planes of his face, in the sinewy muscle of the arms that held her so securely, in the steel-hard legs on which her weight rested he radiated masculinity.

Her pulse gave an unexplained jump that owed nothing to a shocking experience, and her gaze yielded to the glowing depths of his. His arm had found its way around her to complete the circle again. He gave no indication that he was ready to let her go, and Miranda was surprised to find that she didn't particularly want to be released.

The devastating smile changed slowly as his gaze wandered over her face, lingering on each feature. She couldn't remember ever being subjected to such an attentive study, and she wasn't precisely sure when she began studying him just as closely.

"Your only crime at the moment seems to be

that your house is next door to Donald Webster's." His voice sounded distracted, but it was
low and vibrant, echoing from deep in his chest.

The reverberation, which Miranda could feel
as well as hear, touched a harmonic chord
somewhere inside of her. Her eyes seemed to be
drawn magnetically to the movement of his
mouth as he spoke. His upper lip was straight
with only a slight curve but the lower one was
full and sensual.

"What?" she breathed, not really caring.

"Your neighbor, Mr. Webster. The president's
coming." Jake seemed to be having some trouble making sense, too, as his gaze tangled even
more intensely with hers. Neither of them had
the slightest inclination to look away.

"What?" she repeated.

"Nothing," he said abstractedly. It wasn't an
answer; it was a request for quiet.

Miranda recognized his total absorption because it mirrored her own. Her eyes searched
his as thoroughly as he had searched her person
before, looking into their depths for hidden
symbols, undiscovered essences. The brown
color that circled intense black centers was dap-
pled with other hues, gold and green and tur-
quoise. Clear white contrasted sharply with
heavy dark lashes to frame the whole. He had
the most beautiful eyes she'd ever seen.

She had the most beautiful eyes he'd ever
seen, thought Jake. Washed with tears they
were a deep and mysterious green, but also
clear and glowing like a warm fire. He could

have drowned in their depths, he admitted to himself.

Miranda didn't realize that she'd been holding her breath until her lungs reminded her with a burning sensation. Pursing her lips she let out the air in a slow, careful stream so as not to disturb the delicacy of the moment.

Another smile tugged at his lips. He allowed himself a thorough inventory of her face, his gaze skimming across her forehead, over the burnished copper of her hair, down the small, straight, slightly reddened nose to the full sensuality of her lips, where his eyes lingered with a strange hunger before returning to meet her rather uncertain gaze.

Later Miranda would remember the entire episode as impossible to explain. The silent communication between them was as deep as forever, on a level that denied the need for words. His very essence seemed to enter through her eyes, warming the blood that sang throughout her body. Every vein, every nerve throbbed with understanding, until the message finally converged in the focus of her femininity, startling that center of desire with an unexpected electric excitement.

When he spoke again she knew that he shared the same intense craving. "Do you know how tempting you are?" he murmured huskily.

"Am I?"

"Especially your mouth." He started to bend to the temptation.

"I might scream," she warned distractedly.

He frowned.

Miranda was unhappy with his frown. She wanted it to disappear, to be replaced by his smile again. She didn't question her action as she lifted her face toward his. "On the other hand, I might not."

A gleam of appreciation darkened his eyes. He chuckled, and his broad shoulders hunched as he lowered his head. The powerful arm behind her back curved her slowly closer, while his other hand came up to touch her face. His fingers rested lightly on her cheek, stroking the downyness of her skin. At first he just touched his lips to hers.

His were cool and firm, and he tasted of mint. With an almost imperceptible pressure of his fingers, he tilted her face to a more convenient angle. The second brush of his lips was slightly more definite.

Anticipation sent Miranda's breath up to close her throat. She let her lashes drift down to hide the impatience she knew was obvious.

As a result, for the second time that afternoon, she had no warning of the assault that was coming, no time to prepare herself for the tender and glorious attack of his third kiss.

His mouth opened completely over her parted lips, his tongue sweeping inside with a boldness that started her senses reeling. He withdrew only to begin the invasion anew from another point. This time his head tilted to give his hungry mouth the advantage of mastery.

She found herself arching toward him in response, her lips moving instinctively, seeking the impossible, trying to deepen a kiss that was immeasurable.

His hand left her cheek to thread sensuously into her hair, supporting her head. The hand behind her back slipped beneath her arm to stroke the outer curve of her breast. The sensitive skin there reveled in the warmth of his touch as he turned her more fully to face him.

Her tongue joined in the sweet exploration, stroking the rough moisture of his and provoking a sound—strangely like a groan—from his throat. Her hand crept to his nape, adding its pressure to bring them even nearer. She tasted the perspiration on his upper lip, slightly salty as it mingled with her own, and wished this kiss never to end. Never.

But, of course, it had to end. A kiss could not last forever, though somehow she knew that the memory would. The hand that was tangled in her hair finally shifted her face away from his mouth into the curve of his neck.

Jake fought for breath. "God!" he whispered when he could speak again. The word was struck with wonder like an invocation. He was stunned at the raw desire that had hit him so suddenly. When was the last time a woman in his arms had provoked such a powerful reaction? What had begun as the opening salvo to a small seduction scene had grown to a full-blown explosion of sensuality that was as unsettling as it was unforeseen.

Miranda was having her own troubles breathing. Her heart, usually beating at an even, regular tempo, threatened to burst from the tension placed on it. The overpowering passion of the kiss had taken her emotions unaware.

They sat where they were for a minute, her face burrowed in his neck, her nostrils inhaling the delicious male scents of soap, after-shave and musk; and he, staring out over her head, his fingers slightly unsteady as he smoothed the bright hair spilling across her shoulders. Neither wanted to end a moment that had been so spontaneously perfect.

At last Jake gave a sigh and a deep, rather forced chuckle. When he spoke he strove valiantly for nonchalance. It was time to take charge again. "I think I should arrest you for trying to bribe an officer of the law."

Her head fell back to his shoulder as though it had always known that resting place. She gave him a puzzled smile.

The warmth in his eyes gradually faded to a look of guarded speculation. "Would you really have written a check to a thief?" Coupled with his withdrawal the question was an unsuccessful attempt at humor.

The spell that had held Miranda so tightly in its grip was broken. In a rush the images all came back to reproach her with embarrassment and long-overdue caution.

Gosh, she thought, *what am I doing? I practically plastered myself all over him!* She pulled free of his arms and stumbled to her feet. Straightening her skirt with shaky hands, she listened to her own voice, which was as unstable as her pulse. "I don't know," she mumbled. "I guess I just said the first thing that came to mind." *Take it lightly. It was the most awesome kiss I've ever experienced, but, oh please, take it lightly.*

Jake got slowly to his feet, shoving his hands into the pockets of the tight jeans. His unwavering regard never left her face. "I really am sorry."

Her heart plunged to her toes. He wasn't going to take it lightly at all. Damn him.

But his voice was determinedly offhand. "I knew that there was a daughter, of course, and that she had red hair, but my first glimpse of you going through that window was not of your hair."

Miranda began to hope that maybe she could get through this without looking and feeling foolish.

"And certainly nobody told me that you had such gorgeous long legs," he added silkily.

She shot him a suspicious glance, and then, at the thought of the picture she must have made, she rolled her eyes and moaned aloud. Taking refuge in petulance she plunged her own hands into the pockets of her wide skirt and demanded, "Why should you know anything at all about me?"

"I'm a Secret Service agent assigned to the presidential detail, Miranda. He's coming from Washington to Sea Island for a visit."

Miranda breathed a sigh of relief and then

sucked it back in again. The sound of her name on his lips for the first time gave her a further jolt.

Vaguely she remembered having read something, during the pressure of grading finals, about the president's visit to Donald Webster, her parents' next door neighbor. Of course Jake would know her name. She wondered what other information he possessed, and got an eerie feeling at the thought. This particular invasion of her privacy was necessary, she conceded—he was her president, too, and she wanted him protected—but it was nonetheless uncomfortable. "Well, he isn't here yet, is he? So what are you protecting?" she snapped.

"I'm part of the advance team. We've been here for a week." He rearranged his stance almost defensively, with his feet planted apart, hands on his hipbones.

Why he should seem defensive was beyond her. *She* was the one who had been investigated. Did he know about Charles? Without a doubt. The hands in her pockets curled into impotent fists.

"What's the matter?" he asked abruptly.

"Nothing's the matter." The man was really dense! "Nice vacation for you," she said sarcastically.

Her snippy tone didn't seem to offend him in the least. "Some vacation. A presidential visit takes a lot of preparation. Not the least of which is communications—my field. The Man can never be more than seconds away from the

communications network. We have to run new
lines—telephone, telegraph.''

He shrugged as if there was much more to it
than that; but he talked as if he was only filling the silence while he tried to fathom her
sudden change of mood. He seemed puzzled,
she thought ruefully, which wasn't surprising.
She didn't understand it either.

Miranda looked at his hard, fit body. The
short-sleeved knit shirt molded easily to his
broad shoulders and the corded muscles in his
arms. She thought idly that if she ever needed
protecting, this would be the kind of man
she'd want on the job. *If* she ever needed it,
which she wouldn't. She straightened to her
full height. "Well, if you've satisfied yourself
that I'm not dangerous, may I be excused?"
Her self-consciousness and embarrassment still
rankled, and she tried to cover them with more
sarcasm. "I do have to get into the house, you
know."

Jake looked at the window with a frown then
moved closer. "There's blood here," he said,
touching the stuccoed wall where her hands
had rested. He rubbed his fingers together.
"Did you cut yourself?"

She had forgotten the cut, the bump on her
head, the scratch on her nose...and no wonder. But she answered casually, "It's nothing.
I'll put something on it later."

"Let me see." Before she could protest he had
her hand in his, palm up, to examine the cut.
Then he looked at her. Gone was the sensual

ardor. Jake Stewart was sincerely and deeply upset at the sight of her blood. The expression in his eyes was one of concern and more, of sorrow. Miranda had never been more than superficially acquainted with any law-enforcement officer, but she would imagine that empathy like his would be rare in a man who held his job.

"I'm sorry, Miranda," he said quietly, rubbing his thumb the length of her index finger and back.

The caress was having a seductive effect on her, and oddly, he didn't even seem to realize that he was doing it. His motion was a mechanical one, a bodily reflex, while his mind was focused elsewhere.

"You can't climb through all that glass again. I'll go," he offered.

She *had* to get her equilibrium back. She withdrew her hand with as much aplomb as she could muster and looked doubtfully at his broad shoulders, measuring them visually against the width of the window. "I'm afraid you wouldn't fit." She hardly recognized her own voice, it sounded so flimsy.

After a long moment spent searching her face, he followed her gaze and acknowledged the truth of her statement with a crooked smile. "I'm afraid you're right."

"But you can boost me up," she suggested, reaching for the sill with a hasty movement.

Jake wouldn't be rushed. He looked at the window and then at her, as though this were a

statistical problem to be solved in the most effi-
cient way. Finally he stepped forward, swung
her up in his arms and aimed her feet at the
opening. "Try it like this. At least you have
shoes on."

It was not the most graceful entrance Miranda had ever made, especially since her entire
body seemed to be trembling in reaction to the
nearness of Jake Stewart. But finally she was inside. Wincing at the sound of crunching glass
under her shoes, she climbed down from the
sink and crossed the room. The back door, just
off the kitchen, opened into a hall, which ran
the length of the house.

Jake's shoulder rested against the frame, his
long arm stretched across the opening. His eyes
were on her, his lips curved in an attractive half
smile. Not until she stepped back did he shift
his gaze to survey the damage in the kitchen behind her with a soft whistle. "You throw a
wicked purse, Miss Woodbarry," he said, shaking his head. "Do you have a broom?"

"Of course, but—"

He straightened and interrupted briskly, "And
a first-aid kit?"

She waved vaguely toward the front of the
house. "In the bathroom."

His large hand rested briefly on her shoulder,
urging her in the direction she had indicated.
"Go get it while I clean this mess up." He
stooped to pick up the largest pieces of glass
from the floor. When she didn't move he raised
his head. "Scoot," he ordered.

"The broom's in here," she said, pointing to a closet. She retrieved her purse and escaped to the hallway.

Pausing at a mahogany commode to switch on a small Chinoiserie lamp, she looked down at her hand. The bleeding had stopped, thanks probably to the tourniquet hold Jake had kept on her arm. The cut wasn't deep but it stung. Her finger traced the same path that his had covered and she thought again of his strange expression.

What a contradiction Jake Stewart was. Strength and sensitivity were a potent combination in any man. Miranda suspected that this one had a double dose of each, but that he kept the softer emotion well buried. When taken in conjunction with his very powerful masculine appeal either would be downright deadly.

She decided that, though it probably wasn't a good idea, she would like to know him better.

The bathroom beneath the staircase had a first-aid kit, but she passed right by and climbed the stairs to her own bath, flipping on lights as she went. She needed a few minutes alone.

2

DESPITE THE AIR CONDITIONING, Miranda's bedroom had the musty smell of a closed house.
Still she experienced a wonderful feeling of
homecoming as she looked around the tradi-
tionally furnished room. She only visited her
parents during school vacations now, and she
was glad that few changes had been made since
her childhood.

Strategically placed moss-green rugs softened
the effect of highly polished floors. The walls
were painted a soft yellow, and an old favorite
Raggedy Ann doll, which she hadn't been able
to pack away, surveyed her from a yellow ging-
ham chaise. Miranda dropped her purse on the
four-poster bed and crossed the room.

Pushing aside yellow ruffled curtains she
opened the two windows that looked out over
the courtyard where her car was parked. Moving to the adjoining wall, she did the same to
the window that had a view of the pool and of
Donald Webster's home.

Lights were burning upstairs in Donald's
coach house, she noted in surprise. The apartment had been empty for years. The Secret Service must be using it now.

Her thoughts swung again like a pendulum to Jake. Downstairs, underneath her very feet, was the most impressive male she had ever met. Before she faced him again she must get these tricky emotions under control. This sudden attraction, coupled with erotic longings inspired by the handsome Secret Service man, both alarmed and excited her. To be truthful, the encounter with Jake Stewart had swept aside her composure like a fragile cobweb. She was unaccustomed to feeling at a loss.

She whirled away from the window and from the descending darkness outside to walk on slightly shaky legs to the bathroom. She turned the cold faucet wide open, letting the water splatter on her hands and her forearms. Leaning over she splashed more of it onto her face, before turning if off and reaching for a towel. Then she straightened and looked at her reflection in the mirror, surprised by the changes that had appeared since the last time she'd looked at herself.

Miranda hadn't reached the age of twenty-eight without appreciating her looks. She wasn't beautiful, she knew that, but she was attractive enough. Her features taken separately were not remarkable, but the way they came together somehow worked, and she was grateful.

Leaning forward she analyzed the variations in her face with an almost scientific detachment. Her eyes, blessed with a thick fringe of lashes, were considerably brighter. The color in her cheeks lent an appealing glow to the porcelain complexion so common in redheads. Her lips were full and crimson, despite the fact that she wore not a smidgen of lipstick. The lower lip was slightly swollen, adding a bit more sensuality to its curve. All in all, a run-in with a handsome man could achieve an effect better, and yet more subtle, than the most careful makeup artist could accomplish. Miranda was not displeased.

"Miranda?" The voice from downstairs startled her.

"Up here," she called, then took a last look in the mirror. Still holding the hand towel, she went through to the bedroom to find him standing at her door with her suitcases in his hands.

"I just followed the lights. Is this where you want your luggage?" he asked politely.

"Yes," she murmured. "Thank you. But it wasn't necessary for you to bring those up." She twisted her already dry hands into the thick terry cloth.

He set both cases on the floor at the foot of her bed. "I had to do something to make up for my inhospitable greeting," he said easily. "But I'm not finished yet."

Miranda wondered what he meant. Was he afraid of being reported for his mistake? Did he want to pacify her in some way? She straightened her spine and spoke briskly. "No making up is necessary."

His brows lifted in surprise, then understanding softened the line of his mouth. He
came toward her.

She stood her ground as he took the towel
from her fingers and dropped it on the floor,
wanting him to touch her again, yet not wanting it. When his hands came down on her
shoulders she was proud that she didn't tremble, didn't flinch. She kept her eyes straight, and
that put them on a level with the open top button of his shirt. Was the hair visible there as
wiry as the hair that she'd felt at the back of his
head? "Please take your hands away," she
asked in a reasonable voice.

"No," he answered, just as reasonably.

"What?" She did look at him then, but his
expression was unreadable.

He turned her around and gave her a light
shove toward the bathroom door. "The first-aid
kit," he reminded. "I want to attend to that cut."

When she returned with the kit he took it
from her hands and looked around the room.
"Over here." He led her to a chair beside the
window and switched on the old-fashioned
floor lamp. "Sit down," he ordered.

Again Miranda was surprised at her own
meekness. She was definitely not used to men
arranging her to suit themselves. She shrugged
and sat. "When did you say the president is
coming?" she asked in an effort to make casual
conversation.

Jake placed the kit on her lap and came down
on one knee beside her. "He'll be here a week

from today. Let's see what the damage is," he said, reaching for her hand to draw it closer to the light. "I don't believe there's any glass in the cut."

Miranda watched his dark head, bent in concentration, while his long fingers probed her hand. He opened the lid of the metal box, and it fell back to rest against her midriff just below her breasts. She exhaled, but carefully, as her eyes widened. "How—how long will he stay?" Her entire body was so sensitive to the nearness of this man that every move he made registered in her nervous system.

"Four days. This may sting." He added the warning offhandedly as he tore open a foil-wrapped packet.

Good, she thought. *A nice painful sting might take my mind off the warmth of your hands.*

The acrid tang of the antiseptic reached her nostrils before she felt its bite. The slight pain did help distract her, but only briefly. As he turned his head to look in the box for a Band-Aid she saw the scratches her nails had made on his cheek and she caught her breath.

He looked up at her, questioning the dismay in her eyes with a crooked grin. "I warned you that it would sting," he said, ripping the protective cover off the bandage strip.

"It's not that," she whispered. "Your face. Where I scratched you." With her free hand she touched the marks lightly. "I really am sorry."

The warm brown eyes forgave her. "You can return the favor," he said lightly, tearing open another packet and handing her a clean swab.

She held his chin in her other hand and dabbed carefully at the streaks of dried blood. "Does it hurt?"

He didn't answer for a moment. "My face doesn't," he said smoothly. "But having you in my arms left me with an ache that I won't soon forget."

She recognized a hint of studied seduction in his voice but it didn't diminish the effect of his words. Damn her redhead's complexion. She felt the warmth climb her chin to flood her face.

"That's nice," Jake murmured, catching her gaze in the depths of his.

"What is?" she snapped.

"Your blush. I thought it was a lost art." He cupped the back of her head in his big palm and leaned forward the few inches it took to close the gap between their mouths.

Miranda knew she shouldn't allow him to but she was still curious about this man. This kiss was very different from the ones they had shared on the back steps. His mouth was mobile on her lips, tasting their curve, exploring their shape. Assured and experienced, his lips were still tentative, giving her every opportunity to withdraw.

She finally accomplished the seemingly impossible feat, moving her head back to break the contact. "More making up?" she questioned. The words that were supposed to come out as a demand ended up sounding very hoarse and affected.

His eyes sparkled in response. "Miranda, I didn't kiss you to keep you from filing a complaint against me or to try to make up for anything. I kissed you because I wanted to." His knuckles brushed the side of her neck as he pushed her hair behind her shoulder and smiled tenderly at her. "Correction. I had to," he murmured, the black brows knit in a strange frown. His hand lingered to tangle in her hair.

"I know," she answered softly.

"You do?" That surprised him. His brows climbed, and his lips curved into a half smile.

"Yes," she admitted with total honesty. "My suspicion only lasted for half a second. Then I realized you wouldn't do something like that. We've only just met. It doesn't make sense, but I knew."

His hands began an unconscious caress, and the modest smile spread, warming his eyes to the color of toast. His palms rotated at the points of her shoulders, and his long fingers clenched and opened alternately. "It's unusual to find a woman so honest about her feelings."

Miranda went on, trying not to be stirred by the gentle massage. "Just as you know that I wouldn't complain to anyone when you were just doing your duty. Don't you?"

Brown eyes searched her green ones for a long time, then Jake gave himself a mental shake. This woman was so different from any he'd ever known. Didn't she know she was supposed to be evasive and teasing? She was supposed to coax and flirt and pretend indifference, and then he would overcome her objections by seduction and design.

He cut off his thoughts and reached for the first-aid kit in her lap. When he closed the lid his fingers brushed her breast. His hand froze for an endless moment before he stood abruptly and snapped the metal box shut. "I know that you're—" He broke off, unsure himself what he'd been about to say, and pulled her up from the chair into his arms, wrapping them around her securely. His chin rested on the top of her head.

It was a paternal sort of embrace, and Miranda was a bit surprised by it, confused that she could take comfort from a man she'd known so briefly but explosively.

"You're an exceptional woman, do you know that, Miranda Woodbarry?"

"Exceptional?" she questioned, her voice muffled in his chest.

"Um-hm. You don't even know me, and with all you've been through at my hands you can still forgive me."

Underneath her flattened palms she could feel the steady beat of his heart. He was an exceptional man, too. Now that the sensual tension between them seemed to be under control, temporarily at least, she felt an imp of mischief wiggle inside her.

It had been a long, long time since Miranda had felt the urge to flirt. She grinned into his shirt. "I didn't say I forgave you. I only said I wouldn't complain to your boss."

Jake leaned away to look down at her. The smile became a full-blown grin. "Then I wonder if dinner would soften your hard little heart into forgiveness?"

"Dinner?" She had forgotten how hungry she was.

"We could go to The Plantation on St. Simons. They have very good seafood."

She didn't even hesitate. Her eyes glowed in anticipatory delight as she pulled out of his arms. "Wonderful! I haven't eaten since breakfast and I'm starving."

"That certainly produced a positive reaction. Am I to take it as an acquittal?" he teased.

"Call it a deferment. Would you wait while I shower and change?" she asked carefully. "I've been in these clothes all day."

"Sure," he answered. "I'll go next door and get my car." He grinned. "And my wallet, unless you'd like to pay."

"Go get both. My car's air conditioning isn't working, and *you* invited *me* to dinner." It was amazing that her exhaustion had been completely displaced by the prospect of spending more time with him. "I'll hurry."

"Eager, huh?"

She turned him toward the door and gave him a push. "No, just hungry," she corrected. She slammed the door on his back. She could still hear him chuckling as she hurriedly stripped off her clothes and headed for the bath.

3

MIRANDA WAS GRATIFIED to notice that Jake's smile came more easily over dinner. The conversation between them flowed without effort and without any of those awkward silences that usually occur when two people don't know each other well. She found herself comfortable in his company, and the fact relieved her. Comfortable wasn't the word she would have used to describe her feelings a short while ago.

He had roused sensibilities she'd thought were well buried—instant, adolescent-type passions. Maturity should have dispelled that kind of emotion. Now she rationalized that her initial reaction must have been brought on by anxiety, exhaustion and hunger, plain and simple.

As she watched, he took a last bite of Oysters Alfonzo and looked around for the waiter. The man was at his elbow immediately.

"Will you have coffee, Miranda?" Jake asked.

"No, thank you. I'll just finish my tea."

"One coffee," he told the waiter, then he turned back to her, his eyes lingering for a long moment on her lips. The wait for her to shower and change had been well worth it, he decided.

Her white linen slacks were freshly pressed and the jade-green silk blouse was a perfect complement to her hair and eyes. The way the fabric clung to her high breasts afforded him a sharp pleasure.

"You said you teach speech and drama. Do you act yourself?" he asked hurriedly.

She nudged her plate away from the edge of the table and she crossed her arms on the table. Shrugging her shoulders with a tiny movement she smiled teasingly. "On occasion, when the Little Theater in Athens can't find a Kate for *Taming of the Shrew.* I do that one particularly well."

His laugh was a deep rumble, very pleasant, she decided. He relaxed in his chair, one arm hooked casually across its back, his other hand resting motionless on the table. There was an absence of unnecessary movement in this man. No fidgeting, no restless stirring marred his complete self-possession.

"Was it she who cursed me so thoroughly this afternoon?"

"With a few of my own embellishments."

"Shameful language for a lady," he admonished, trying unsuccessfully to control the twitching of his lips.

"I know," she agreed with a grin. With one hand she cupped her chin and drummed her fingers against her cheek. "But strongly provoked."

He was silent, neither denying nor affirming the light accusation, his attention riveted on the movement of her fingers. From there it was a very short distance to her mouth, where his gaze lingered for a heart-stopping moment before lifting to lock in on her eyes. A sudden tension vaulted between them like an electric arc. Miranda was stunned by its charge and overwhelmed by the desire it sparked. Damn! She had congratulated herself too soon.

The waiter's white-sleeved arm accomplished what she could not—breaking their visual connection as he set Jake's coffee cup in front of him. By the time the black brew had been poured, cream and sugar offered and refused and the man had left, Miranda had regained some of her composure.

She stirred restlessly in an effort to dispel the sensual atmosphere that lingered and curled her fingers into a loose fist against her cheek. Finally she sat back in her chair, consciously withdrawing from his nearness. She started to reach for the tall glass of iced tea and changed her mind. Her shaking hand probably couldn't hold it.

"Actually I prefer teaching and directing to acting," she said hurriedly. "And I've been blessed with some very talented pupils. I have two former students on one of the daytime soaps, and one appeared briefly in a miniseries last year."

"So you've never tried Broadway or Hollywood?"

She laughed lightly at the suggestion. "Heavens no! I haven't the least ambition to become a professional. The academic life suits me fine."

"Yet I have the idea that you could do anything you set your mind to." Candlelight flickered over his rough-hewn features, highlighting a mysterious gleam in his eyes.

Miranda let her lashes hide her expression. It was the nicest kind of compliment and it helped to blunt her uneasiness.

Jake watched the soft fan of her lashes shadow her cheeks and thought what a seductively feminine woman she was. Her self-confidence had returned, and with it her balance and poise. She was witty and intelligent, and he was surprised at how much he was enjoying himself.

The Plantation was one of his favorite places to eat on the island. Popular because of its superb food, it still managed to provide a serene and quiet atmosphere, suiting his motives perfectly. Miranda had seconded his choice. Their meal had lasted for more than an hour because they had stopped eating so often to talk. But talk wasn't Jake's primary reason for bringing her here.

He wanted Miranda Woodbarry in his bed. His decision was sudden and probably totally irrational, but she was warm and alluring and utterly desirable. He wanted her with an intensity that surprised him, and would probably petrify her. She beguiled him, tempted him to feel things he'd never known before, things that were dangerous to his well-being. He was more used to conquest than courtship.

Jake had lived by the philosophy that a

woman's affections were like guarded trea-
sures. If a woman intrigued him he simply had
to find the right combination and she would
open to him on oiled hinges, with barely a
squeak. And when Jake Stewart wanted a woman, he could be very patient in his search for the
right key.

But under the warmly charming appeal of
Miranda Woodbarry that philosophy seemed to
be undergoing a subtle change. Determinedly
he kept his gaze away from the firm uptilted
thrust of her breasts against green silk. He took
a swallow of coffee and ignored the warning in
his mind.

She, too, sipped at her drink, leaving a gloss
of moisture on her lower lip. With an unconscious delicacy of movement she touched the
spot with a corner of her napkin. "Is this your
first trip to Sea Island?" she asked.

He grabbed on to the subject, hoping to de-
tour the conversation to a safe, even common-
place channel. "Yes. It's beautiful down here,
and perfect for a presidential visit."

At her curious glance he went on to explain,
"The long causeway that leads to the island is
an ideal lookout point. There's no other access
except by water, and of course the Coast Guard
will patrol the sea."

"I grew up in Macon but we spent every
summer here. I loved the island for the same
reason. Because it was so safe my parents let me
roam wherever I wanted." She smiled and her
eyes took on a reminiscent gleam.

Jake was shocked at the jealousy that coursed through him. He felt like she'd deserted him for her memories. Hell! He had to quit this. These feelings were too quick, too uncontrollable. He leaned forward in his chair. It was his turn to fold his arms on the table. Against his better judgment he shifted the low, fat candle to the side and reached for her hand.

She didn't protest but she didn't respond either. Her fingers lay passive, hesitant in his. When she spoke it was with false brightness.

"I seem to have been doing all the talking. Tell me about you, Jake." She cleared her throat before continuing. "Where are you from? Do you have family?"

"My stepfather lives near Detroit. I never knew my real father, who died before I was born. My mom passed away six years ago."

"Are you an only child, too?"

He nodded. "I'm very close to my stepfather. We take a long vacation together every year. He's retired now . . . ." His words trailed off abstractedly. "You and I are very different, Miranda," he said quietly.

"Well, I probably seem provincial to you. You live in Washington. Your job takes you all over the world."

"It goes deeper than that. You're a product of a certain kind of life-style, background. I'm the result of another."

What did he mean, wondered Miranda. Was he talking about the elegance of her parents' home on Sea Island? Jake didn't seem uncomfortable in the luxurious setting, but then she knew very little about his own background. Maybe with this man her parents' wealth and position were a handicap. The idea struck her as funny. Charles had been attracted to her because of her parents' money, yet it seemed to bother Jake.

What his father did certainly didn't matter to her. "Was your stepfather in the automotive business? That's what I always think of when Detroit is mentioned."

"In a related line," he answered evasively. Her skin was so soft. He traced a fine blue vein in her wrist with his thumb and watched her swallow in response. She was as aroused as he was. So why didn't he move on her? What was holding him back? "Is there an important man in your life, Miranda?" he asked before he could stop himself.

The green eyes widened at the sudden change of topic. Their vivid color darkened. "I was married once. It didn't work out."

He waved a dismissive hand. "I know about that. I mean now."

Of course Jake would know that she'd been married, thought Miranda. Anyone who knew her would furnish that information and other juicy facts besides. She wondered how deeply the Secret Service had delved into her personal life. Had they interviewed Charles's mistresses?

"I'm surprised you haven't found that out, too. I thought you were supposed to know everything," she added quietly but with a hint of irritation.

"You were very young," he said simply, seeming to read beyond the slight sarcasm in her voice.

"Yes. Very young, very naive and very stupid." She forced herself to smile despite the unhappy memories his question had evoked. "Our backgrounds were very much alike, my husband's and mine, and look what happened."

"You were well out of it."

"I know," she said quietly. "I'm sorry. It isn't your fault that you have to snoop."

His brows snapped together. The fingers that had held hers loosely now contracted until their grip was almost painful. She was again faced with the image of the iron-hard, no-nonsense man who had pulled her so ungraciously from the window. That man had disappeared for a while, but now he was back.

"I don't apologize for my job, Miranda. It may have unsavory aspects, but unfortunately in this day and age it's completely necessary," he ground out.

"Of course it is, Jake. I didn't mean to make light of what you do." Miranda was embarrassed at how stiff the apology sounded. "I really am sorry," she added, trying again to inject the sincerity she felt.

Why did she feel compelled to erase that look from his eyes, that harshness from his features? She was startled to acknowledge her stinging discomfort at the sight of his scowl, remembering the moment before he'd kissed her for the first time and how unhappy she'd been at his frown.

She barely knew this man. During dinner she'd relaxed in his company, and it was a nice feeling. She hadn't enjoyed a man so much in years, but why should a glower on his face cause her distress? Logically her reaction should have been annoyance, and she was annoyed with herself that it was not.

Something in her expression must have convinced him that she was suitably chastized, for his brow finally cleared and he smiled again. "I did give you a hard time, didn't I?"

She grinned back, if reluctantly. "You certainly did. I've never been searched—or is it frisked—before."

His low husky chuckle sent a trail of shivers down her spine. She watched, fascinated, as his eyes slowly deepened from brown to almost black. "I won't apologize for that either. It's part of the job," he said easily. But a twinkle lurked in those dark eyes. The grip on her hand shifted, and he entwined their fingers. Never releasing her eyes he lifted her hand to let his lips play softly across her knuckles.

Miranda's heart slowed to a heavy beat. The warmth of his breath on her hand had a sensual effect like none she'd ever known.

"Would you like something else? Dessert?" he asked, but his expression asked far more.

"No, thank you." She shook her head as she

speculated whimsically on the connection between them. A thread of awareness seemed to have been spun into a strange magical web that somehow held them both captive. The sensation was not one-sided; of that she was convinced. He was as conscious of its presence as she.

As though he had read her thoughts, seen into her mind, Jake smiled. His lids drooped slightly, and his voice touched her like a caress. "I'm about to do something I've never done before, Miranda."

"Oh? And what is that?"

Instead of answering he signaled for the check. How cold her hand felt when he released it.

The waiter's response was immediate. Jake glanced at the total and reached into his pocket for some bills.

"Thank you, sir. Come back to see us."

"We will," Jake assured the man. He stood and came around the table to pull out her chair. When they were outside he took Miranda's hand again. He kept it firmly in his, palm to palm, fingers entwined, as they strolled toward his car.

The heat of the day had cooled to a pleasant balmy temperature, and a heavy yellow moon hung low in the indigo sky. The scent of jasmine in the air, the clasp of Jake's fingers threatened to reawake the feelings she'd had earlier. The night suddenly was ethereal and filled with magic.

"You know, Miranda, you almost make me believe in things I know don't exist."

"Ummm?" she hummed rather dreamily.

"Like romance and love."

The words were a dash of cold water on her psyche. She didn't take offense at them—indeed she didn't know him well enough to understand what prompted his severe outlook. They just made her sad. Deliberately she tugged her hand free and moved a step in front of him as they approached his gray sedan. "What is it you're going to do that you've never done before?" she asked brightly.

"Please hear me out, okay?"

She nodded. He started to open the door, changed his mind and shoved both hands into the pockets of his jeans. He glanced down at his feet before meeting her eyes.

The entire incident was so at variance with what she was learning about this man that her curiosity was piqued. "Is something wrong, Jake?" she asked softly.

His free hand came up to tuck a strand of hair behind her ear, and his fingers lingered at her neck. "No . . . that is . . . . To tell you the truth I don't know how to handle the feelings I'm having about you. If you were any other woman I would be wondering how quickly I could get you into bed. With you, however, I want to be truthful. Any committed relationship is impossible between us." He paused. "But you are one hell of a sexy woman, Miranda Woodbarry."

She blanched at the raw honesty. He was here

on a temporary mission; he was reminding her of that. She should have been reminding herself. While there was no point in denying the attraction between them, she didn't plan to be a temporary diversion for anyone. She reached behind her for the handle to the car door. "And you're a sexy man, but if I try very hard, maybe I can manage to resist your charms," she said, meaning to deliver the words humorously. Instead they came out seriously.

Jake's hand stopped the movement when she would have closed the door behind her. He leaned one elbow on the frame and looked down at her with an expression of pure enjoyment. "Miranda, don't get prickly. I have no intention of throwing you to the ground and making violent love to you the first night we meet." The dimple in his cheek appeared, then vanished, then appeared again. He was trying not to laugh.

All of a sudden she wanted to laugh with him. She could take this attraction as lightly as he. "Jake, listen. I arrived this afternoon with no air conditioning in my car, tired from the rush of finals, angry because I was locked out and hungry. The added burden of being suspected of sedition hasn't helped. I'm not usually this malleable."

"I didn't think you were."

She ignored his interruption. "I'll admit to a certain curiosity about you. And a certain ... ah, interest. But I'm not a naive girl. I have no intention of hopping into bed with you because you're an attractive man." She smiled, pleased at how reasonable her speech sounded.

He closed the door on her warning and circled the car to get in beside her. When they were on the road he grinned and spoke again, scattering her wits. "But I want you," he said as casually as if he'd been commenting on the weather.

Her eyes swung to him. The muscle that jumped in his jaw belied his casual tone. He meant every word of it. Her pulse gave a funny leap.

"There is no point in denying the fact. And we're going to be living next door to each other for almost two weeks," he added.

She turned sideways in the seat, her back to the door in order to watch him more closely. "Oh? Are you staying with Donald, too?" Her voice was calm and composed, she noted with satisfaction.

"We're using the apartment over the garage."

"That's right, I noticed the lights."

"And I noticed that your bedroom window looks right into mine. You'd better be careful when you undress," he teased.

"I'm always careful about that," she said sweetly. "But I'm sure you are too much of a gentleman to take advantage if I forget."

"Miranda, I wouldn't want you to think you don't excite me every time I look at you. So just to keep the record straight, I said I didn't *intend* to make love to you tonight, not that I didn't *want* to. I plan to use every device I can think of to break through your defenses."

Her laugh sounded breathless to her ears, and she only hoped it didn't sound that way to him. "Is that a threat?" she asked, wondering why she wasn't furious at the arrogant assumption that she'd go along with his plans. She tilted her head to study him in the faint light from the dash and answered her own question. She wasn't furious, simply because there was no arrogance in his expression, just total self-confidence. She couldn't prevent the second small laugh that escaped.

"A threat? I'd prefer to think of it as a statement of desire—desire stronger and more baffling than I've ever known."

She shook her head helplessly, not believing this conversation but not able to disbelieve it either. "You're very generous to put me on notice like this." And amazing, she added silently. "The number of women who fall for that line must be staggering."

"Uh-uh. You're forgetting the original subject of this conversation."

His voice sounded a little strained and she wondered why. *She* was the one besieged.

"I've never been this honest with a woman before."

"I'm honored." Miranda pinched a pleat in her slacks between her fingers up and down from midthigh to knee. "I'll give some thought to your proposition. Would you mind stopping at the all-night market on the way back? I need a few things for breakfast."

Jake's voice was completely neutral as he accepted her change of subject. "Of course not," he said.

JAKE STOOD AT THE WINDOW in his sun-splashed room the next morning and looked across the expanse of lawn, broken only by the sparkling blue pool, to the house next door. The apartment over the garage was on the edge of the Webster property and only fifty or sixty feet from Miranda's bedroom window.

He had stood in this very spot last night and watched her lower the window shade with a firm and decisive hand. When her light finally went out he'd watched her raise it again.

On impulse he had reached for the telephone and punched her number, already stored in a corner of his mind.

"Hello." She had sounded tolerant, and he grinned in the darkness.

"I thought you might be interested in knowing about a device that the army came up with a few years ago," he said without preamble. "It's now standard equipment for Secret Service details."

"Jake, what on earth are you talking about?" she asked with a tired sigh.

"This particular piece of equipment was developed for night reconnaisance. It looks just like any other pair of binoculars—" He winced when she slammed the phone down in his ear, but gave a satisfied grunt as he watched her jerk down the shade again.

He smiled to himself. When he'd told her that she excited him, it might have been the understatement of the year. He could hardly remember the feeling, so long had it been since he'd reacted to a woman as he had to her.

Women abounded in Washington, beautiful women, available women, and some not so much available as willing. He'd had his share. But this woman was different; he couldn't put his finger on the reason. She was beautiful, intelligent and self-confident without being egotistical. Fresher, somehow new, despite the fact that she'd been married. Perhaps it was a lack of bitterness; no shell surrounded her. In going through her divorce, she had coped admirably with an unhappy situation that she was well out of.

That turkey, Springer, her former husband, had gotten careless. If he'd wanted to marry for money he should at least have kept his wife happy. But he'd gone from one affair to another until finally it was inevitable that someone would tell her.

Jake could imagine Miranda's reaction, at nineteen years old and faced with betrayal only a few short months after a huge society wedding. What was it in her character that had enabled her to recover without the scar of bitterness? Whatever it was, it was refreshing.

He'd fallen asleep with Miranda Woodbarry on his mind, and he awoke with her there several times during the night. By the time morning dawned he was filled with anticipation at the thought of seeing her again. He showered and shaved, humming to himself.

Miranda might pretend otherwise but he knew the signs. She wanted him, too. The prospect of the next two weeks began to look brighter every minute.

"Jake, have you worked out the code names for this trip?" The voice came from his bedroom door.

"No, Andy." He turned from the window, his thoughts reverting immediately to the matter at hand. The beautiful woman next door faded from his mind, as though she'd never been there. Or to be more correct she was shut into a separate compartment, one that he could close off completely until he was ready to open it again.

Miranda awoke refreshed and unusually expectant. Recognizing the source of her good mood was easy, as she turned her head on the pillow to look toward the window. She smiled, remembering Jake's call. He hadn't had to warn her. What was it about him that could spark more anticipation than she'd felt for years? She stretched her arms over her head, arching her back like a cat, then bounced out of bed in one exuberant motion before heading for the shower.

The warm water pelted her body while scraps of memory pelted her senses—the taste of his lips, his scent, the feel of his hand at her waist. After turning out her light last night she had allowed her thoughts to return to him. In her fantasy she had pictured him peeling off his jeans, stripping the shirt over his head, muscles rippling as he slid between clean sheets. Had he crossed his hands beneath his head as she'd done? Had he lain there thinking of her? Did he wear pajamas or sleep in the raw? Somehow she had the idea he probably slept naked.

After drying her body, Miranda slipped on her last year's bathing suit—standard uniform for summer days on the island—and a thigh-length cover-up. Twisting her unruly copper-colored hair into a careless topknot, she descended the stairs with a skip.

The beach beckoned through the French doors at the foot of the staircase but she resisted for now, turning instead toward the back of the house.

She prepared the electric percolator with water and a measured amount of coffee grounds, all the while humming softly to herself. As she attached the cord she glanced up to see the white curtains move in the breeze, and she winced.

The man who answered at the Sea Island Company was not pleased when she reported a broken window, but he promised to send someone over right away. When the knock came only moments later she was in the small laundry room off the kitchen, searching for the supply of beach towels her mother kept there. "It's open," she called.

"Good morning."

She whirled at the sound of the deep voice, one hand going to her breast to quiet her pounding heart. "You startled me."

Jake stood at the door to the tiny room, one hand on either side of the frame, and grinned at her surprise. "Who were you expecting?"

She hadn't remembered his being this large. Or was it the small, confined space? His bulk filled the doorway like another wall, and she felt a suffocating intimacy between them, which, when she paused to think about it, wasn't altogether unpleasant. A smile spread across her features. "A man to fix the window. Good morning."

The dimple dug deeper into his cheek. He allowed his eyes to slip briefly down her body to her bare legs and back up to her features, lingering longest at her lips. "You look good in the morning," he murmured.

He looked good, too. The healthy tan, the clear eyes almost as dark as his hair, the straight white teeth all contributed to his overwhelmingly masculine presence, which seemed to flow from him like a cloud, filling the room and her senses. She felt a warm hand grip her midsection and fingers of warmth spread throughout her body setting up a tingle all the way to her bare toes. She leaned against the washer, not sure whether she wanted to appear nonchalant or whether she needed the support.

He was dressed casually again, in jeans and a kelly-green polo shirt. "So do you," she told him honestly, if a little huskily.

The remark surprised him. "Thanks."

Her eyes narrowed as she noticed the scratches along his cheekbone. The marks were no longer red and puffy but they still looked angry. "Does your face hurt?"

"Not a bit," he answered. "How is your hand?"

She held it up for his inspection. "The Band-Aid came off in the shower, and I decided to leave it off."

He leaned forward slightly to look but didn't leave his post at the door. "I'm glad there wasn't any permanent damage." His eyes returned to hers and neither of them spoke for a moment.

Finally Miranda dragged her wayward thoughts away from his sensuality. "Would you like some coffee?" she offered. "I just fixed a pot."

"I'd like . . . coffee, yes," he murmured suggestively. Clearly coffee was not what he meant.

As she approached she had the uncanny feeling that he wasn't going to let her pass, but then he took a step back. "You're not working today?" she asked lightly as she moved before him into the kitchen. The percolator, warmed now, gave a gurgle, paused, then bubbled again.

"As a matter of fact, I'm here on business."

"Business?" Miranda was pleased that her voice held just the right amount of interest. She opened a cabinet door and took down two bright-blue mugs. The tingle intensified at the back of her neck, and she half turned to face him. "What kind of business?" He was very close.

She just had time to set the mugs down before she felt his lips on her nape, cool and gentle. A finger traced her hairline and tugged lightly at a curl that had escaped its confinement. "Is this the beginning of your campaign of seduction?"

"Um-hm," he murmured against her skin.

"You said you came on business," she choked. She should never have spent so much time daydreaming about him. Her dreams were pale in comparison to having him here in the flesh. The passion he could so easily kindle in her now threatened to consume all her good intentions to go slow.

His arms folded around her waist and tugged her back into the cradle of his hips. "Business can wait and so can coffee. You never did answer my question last night," he said into her hair.

Miranda licked dry lips and swallowed. "What question?" she breathed. His forearms rested beneath the lower curve of her breasts stimulating a hunger to have him touch her, to feel his broad palms cover her fullness and lift her in a tender massage. The coffee was bubbling frantically in the tiny glass dome, but it was no more agitated than the heated blood in her veins.

She let her head fall back against his shoulder, her eyes, drowsy with desire, meeting his.

"I'm not sure I want it answered." He dipped his head to cover her lips in a soft kiss. "It doesn't seem to matter anymore." His tongue probed the corner of her mouth, teasing her, coaxing a response that, if he had only known, she was more than ready to give.

Her lips parted, and her own tongue joined the play. The effect on him was electric. A harsh moan escaped his throat, vibrating against her mouth, and his hands came up to embrace her breasts through the fabric of her bathing suit and the cover-up, moving hungrily in a circular pattern until she arched into their touch. His fingers brushed the hardened tips of her nipples.

Suddenly she could stand no more. She needed to feel his length against her. She turned in his arms and pressed closer, letting him take her weight. Her arms wound around his neck, her hands sliding into the dark thickness of his hair.

He caught her in a hard grasp, his mouth hovering for a moment before swooping down to bury hers in a kiss of infinite hunger. While one broad hand held her steady, his hips ground against hers, leaving her with no doubt that his desire was as great as her own.

When he finally broke off the kiss he was breathing like a long-distance runner. He rested his damp forehead on hers, taking great breaths before he found his voice. "I want to look at you," he whispered. It was not a request or even a demand, but a simple statement of fact. He moved one hand between them, retaining his pressure at the small of her back with the other.

Very slowly he pulled one end of the sash of her beachcoat until the bow fell apart. He spread both sides away, one at a time, still moving with almost painful slowness. Then he was gazing with fixed absorption at the generous curve of her breasts between the V-neck of her maillot. They swelled immediately and her nipples hardened in response, as though he'd touched them with more than his eyes. His gaze skittered to her neck, where he found what he was seeking. He released the tie strap and the top of her suit fell to her waist.

His ragged sigh was one of relief, as though he had been afraid that at any moment she might stop him. Miranda wondered dazedly why she hadn't.

The hand at her back began to move in a warm circle, as did his other hand on the curves of her breasts. His touch was as light as down. "I dreamed about this last night," he rasped hoarsely. "I woke up at three in the morning covered in a cold sweat, wanting you, aching for you. You are more beautiful than my dreams."

She caught her breath every time those long fingers came close to her nipples, but he avoided the places that ached for his touch. "Please, Jake," she whispered.

"Please what, honey? Please touch you like this?" His thumb and forefinger caught the rosy peak in a gentle nip. She gasped at the sensation. "Or like this?" His large hand swallowed her breasts and squeezed lightly. He bent his head to take one hard nipple into his mouth, rolling his tongue around it and using his teeth and his lips to drive her further toward total oblivion.

He finally lifted his head to look down at her with a softly blurred expression. She was breathing through her mouth, when she could breathe at all, and her lips and throat were as arid as a desert. She rimmed her lips with her tongue in a desperate effort to moisten them. His tongue was there immediately in response to her need.

"Miranda," he groaned into her mouth. "Lord, you're beautiful. I want you so much I'm shaking with it! Let me take you upstairs."

Upstairs? The word went off like a warning signal in Miranda's brain. Dear God, what was she doing? She wedged her arms between them, flattening her palms on his chest in an effort to push away from the desire that gripped her. His mouth moved to the skin of her throat, finding the pulse there with his tongue. The rapid-fire heartbeat under her hands testified to his arousal as blatantly as did his maleness, pressed against her stomach. She wanted him, too; wanted to say, yes, take me upstairs. "No, Jake," she finally managed, but it was a weak protest, much too weak for a woman of maturity and sense.

The sound of a truck outside brought both of them back to reality. Jake lifted his head to peer beyond her shoulder. He shook his head a little as though to clear his thoughts, as though he had forgotten everything outside the circle of her arms. When he spoke, the words were an accusation. "The man's here to fix the window."

"I told you he was coming," she whispered.

"I know. It seemed to have slipped my mind for some reason." He rested his forehead again on hers and smiled. If the smile was rather shaky, it was all the more endearing to Miranda. She touched his cheek with one hand.

Jake covered her hand with his and turned his face into her palm to plant a soft kiss there. "I'll let him in, honey. Go fix your suit."

She looked at him doubtfully, but he turned her to the door of the hall just before she heard a footstep on the gravel driveway.

She glanced over her shoulder to see Jake jam one hand into the pocket of his jeans and reach for the now silent percolator with the other. He lifted the pot to pour a stream of dark-brown liquid into one of the blue mugs.

She let the door swing shut behind her and took a long, deep breath. Her fingers were clumsy and awkward with the strings of her bathing suit, but she finally managed to get them tied.

Instead of returning to the kitchen, she unlocked the doors overlooking the beach and walked out onto the tiled veranda that ran the length of the house. The cushions for the heavy iron furniture hadn't been unpacked but she hardly noticed the hardness of the chair she perched on. She hunched her shoulders, leaning her weight on the heels of her hands, and tried to think.

Jake found her there a few minutes later. "He measured the window. Now he's gone to cut the glass." When she didn't answer he crossed to the balustrade and leaned against it, facing her. He folded his arms over his broad chest and crossed his legs at the ankles. "He said he'd be back in about an hour."

She risked a glance at him and wished she hadn't. His expression was filled with tenderness, and his eyes held a tiny flame, a remnant of the passionate scene a few minutes ago. "Thank you." She rose impatiently to her feet and plunged her fists into the pockets of the beachcoat. "Jake, I...."

"Miranda...."

They spoke together and laughed together, though Miranda's laughter was strained.

"You first," he offered.

She avoided his eyes as she strolled over to prop her forearms on the stone balustrade beside him. Linking her fingers lightly she stared out to sea for a moment before she began. It was with some difficulty that she searched for the right words. "I know that you probably.... I don't want you to think that I fall into the arms of every good-looking man I meet, like I have yours." The last phrase came out in a rush. "You are very practiced, very experienced." She took in a long breath and let it out again. "I'm not sure that I want to get involved with you."

Jake looked down at her bent head. "Maybe

it's time you answered my question," he said quietly.

She finally met his eyes. "What question?"

"The question about a man in your life. Is there anyone important, Miranda?"

She turned cold at the inference. How could he possibly believe a thing like that of her? She straightened and fixed him with a sparkling green glare. "I don't know what kind of women you usually associate with, Mr. Stewart. Do you think that if there were anyone else I would have let you kiss me, much less . . . ?" She sputtered, unable to finish.

He caught her arm when she would have stalked away indignantly. She wouldn't give him the satisfaction of struggling this time. But she looked pointedly at the long fingers that detained her, and they fell away.

"Touch you?" he finished for her. "I'm not particularly familiar with this kind of situation either, Miranda." He leaned his hip against the balustrade and folded his arms across his chest. "I've never wanted a woman as quickly or as completely as I want you. My feelings for you have me off balance. I'm not sure I know how to handle them."

Her features softened somewhat at the confession. She had an idea that there weren't many things that caught him off balance. "Do you have to handle them anyway, Jake?"

He gave her a rueful grin. "I'm too much in the habit of planning ahead. Perhaps it comes from my training. Preventive measures are the most important part of my job, and they seem to spill over into my everyday life, too."

"You sound as though you feel you need protection from me." Her brow furrowed. She took up a stance facing him, watching her hand sweep absently across the slight roughness of the stone.

His voice was deep and warm and very sensual when he answered. "I have an idea, beautiful lady, that you may be the most dangerous person I've ever run into."

"Then we probably *should* avoid each other," she stated, looking up into his unrevealing expression.

"Like the plague," he concurred, holding her gaze.

Miranda felt a shiver of disappointment, but she shrugged and crossed her arms against its chill. "We're agreed then," she said heavily. "We won't see each other while you're here." It was for the best, she told herself.

He ran an exasperated hand through his thick hair. "Hell, yes, we're going to see each other!"

"But you said...."

"Forget that. I've said a lot of crazy things in the short time I've known you, Miranda. You've got me in a tailspin and I hardly know *what* I'm saying. But I do know that we're not saying goodbye!"

"BUSINESS," MIRANDA REMINDED JAKE as she stripped bacon from the package and arranged it in the copper-bottomed skillet.

"Ah, yes. Business before pleasure." He opened a carton of eggs. His arm brushed against hers.

"Or instead of pleasure," she told him shortly as she moved out of his way. They had agreed to shelve the discussion of their mutual attraction for the present, or at least until after breakfast.

Jake seemed to have developed a sudden case of clumsiness. He had to catch Miranda's waist to steady himself as he reached into a cabinet above her head for a bowl. He took advantage of the opportunity to nibble at her neck.

"Jake!" she warned. She slid the skillet to a back burner and turned, fully intending to glare at him. But his apologetic smile was so meek and so blatantly false that she gave up and laughed. "You are too obvious."

He tried unsuccessfully to tone down his grin and held up an egg. "How many?" he asked.

"One."

He broke four eggs into the heavy pottery bowl and picked up a wire whisk before he spoke again. "We would like your permission to station a guard at the entrance to your driveway."

"And if I don't choose to give it?" Miranda pulled the electric juicer forward and began to halve fresh oranges.

He shrugged, poking at the eggs. "We'll do it anyway."

"I thought so." She pressed half an orange against the turning extractor and watched the golden juice flow from the spout. "Why bother to ask?" she asked, raising her voice to be heard over the whirring sound of the appliance.

"Courtesy," he answered loudly. "There's a direct view across your lawn to the gate between the two properties. We can't leave it unguarded. I hope you understand, Miranda."

She was aware of his eyes as they followed her movements but didn't speak again until the pulp of a half dozen oranges had been liquified to her satisfaction and the skins disposed of in the trash compactor. Then she faced him defensively, picking up the conversation with her answer. "Of course I understand. It's just that I don't relish the idea of being virtually under guard myself."

"There'll be no restriction on you. You may go and come as you wish. But your visitors will have to be identified." He hesitated. "I would imagine you have a lot of visitors?"

Her eyes darted to his. "Quite a few," she acknowledged. "I *have* been coming here all my life."

"We'll try not to make them uncomfortable."

"I suppose it's necessary," she said with a sigh as she edged around his bulk to the stove. She picked up a two-pronged fork and turned the bacon. For some reason it was easier to carry on this conversation while her hands were busy and her attention could be diverted by her tasks, diverted from the mental images she retained of violence to other presidents.

She remembered seeing a television news report, horrifying in its immediacy, of when another president had been wounded. Two men had been left bleeding on the ground while Secret Service agents bodily lifted the leader into his waiting limousine. "How does he stand it? Having his every movement watched? It would drive me crazy," she said finally in a small voice.

"He gets impatient sometimes," Jake acknowledged. Suddenly his concentration seemed to be totally on the eggs.

Miranda shot a glance at him. His light mood had turned serious. She wondered at the guarded tone in his voice. Had the president given them the slip on occasion?

Jake went on to explain some of their protection procedures as well as their arrangements for the instant communication that was necessary when the president traveled.

Miranda was awed. "There really is a man with the little black box!" she breathed.

"Certainly. Except it's an attache case," Jake

corrected her. "The president never has the luxury of being incommunicado."

"For heaven's sake! What do you do when he goes out of the country?"

Jake grinned. "Don't ask. It's a nightmare. Most of the Western bloc countries have security systems at least as thorough as ours, but this president seems to pick out the most underdeveloped nations in the world to visit."

"Will you be standing guard while he's here?" she asked as she tucked bread into the slots of the toaster.

"Not unless I'm needed. We have thirty-six agents arriving with the president. They alternate eight-hour surveillance shifts. I only handle the communications."

"Oh, yes. You told me that." She looked around. Everything was ready except for the bacon and eggs, so there was no more busy work to do. Her eyes were worried as they scanned his broad shoulders. "Do you have to wear a gun, too?"

"When the president arrives, not before. We're all armed then."

She didn't want to ask, but she did anyway. "Have you ever been in danger yourself, Jake?"

The muscles across his back tensed. If she hadn't been watching she would not have noticed. He didn't answer for a moment, but when he did she was sorry she'd voiced the question that had been uppermost in her mind since the beginning of the conversation. "Once or twice," he admitted with restraint.

He lifted his head to look through the broken

window. His profile was rigid; his eyes distracted. He gazed inward toward some memory she wouldn't be allowed to share.

"I'm sorry. I didn't mean to bring up a disturbing subject," she said softly.

He shrugged as though to dislodge a weight from his shoulders.

"Tell me more about what you will do here," she urged, hoping to erase the memory that held him in its grip.

Finally his shoulders relaxed, his jaw released from its tight clench, and he shifted his gaze to her face. His expression was still taut, however, as he spoke. "The trip wires that we put in place will be hidden in the shrubbery. You won't be able to see them. We have men stationed at each corner of the property where the president stays, so since there are only two houses in this block, we'll have a total ring of security. Of course the staff preparing Webster's house for the visit are the only ones allowed in right now."

"Well, do whatever you have to do. I have no objections, Jake," she reassured him in the same soft tone.

"Thanks." His features relaxed, but she turned away from the remnant of pain evident there. Something had happened to Jake Stewart in the line of duty, something that had left deep scars on his feelings.

The bacon was done. She arranged it on a folded paper towel to drain and moved out of Jake's way.

He glanced around as though trying to re-member what he was supposed to be doing. Giving the eggs a last swipe with the wisk, he emptied them into the skillet he'd prepared. The hot butter sizzled briefly, then Jake stirred for a few minutes without speaking while Miranda arranged plates, utensils and food on a tray.

When the eggs were done to moist fluffiness he turned them onto the warm platter she had readied. "I have another request," he stated.

She lifted her brows. He sounded more like himself, she thought in quiet relief.

"Do you have one or two friends in Brunswick or St. Simons who might be intrested in doing a little volunteer work?"

She thought for a moment. "Yes, I know several people."

"We like to have local contacts to operate with us on securing clearance for the press."

"What would they have to do?"

"It's mostly manning the telephones for a couple of days. The regulars, the White House correspondents, will be brought in by plane. Of course, they're already cleared, but local and state reporters have to be checked out. We run their social security numbers through our computers and check their press credentials to make sure they're who they say they are. Once the retinue actually arrives the volunteer work would be finished."

Miranda handed him the tray and led the way through the hall to the patio where they had sat earlier. "What about me?" she asked as he placed the tray on a round glass-topped table.

He hesitated for only a moment. Something flashed in his eyes before he spoke. "Fine. You might be coerced into doing some chauffeuring, too. The network press people like to pick up local color for the nightly news."

"I'd love it," Miranda admitted as she began to empty the tray. "A presidential visit is rather exciting, isn't it?"

"And a hell of a lot of work. But we can't expect the chief to stay holed up in one spot for four years." He held her chair for her and circled the table to take the place opposite. "Anyway, you would be ideal since you already have security clearance."

"You mean I'm not a dangerous character?" she asked as she poured orange juice into squat little glasses. She tried to keep the touchiness out of her voice but didn't succeed.

He sighed and shook his head. "No, Miranda. You're not a dangerous character," he answered patiently. "Not to the president anyway."

Her lips pursed, but she didn't say anything.

"We'll need at least one other person to help you. Do you have any friends who you think would be willing?"

"Patricia Sanders might. She lives on St. Simons." She watched as he drew a small notebook from the hip pocket of his jeans and wrote down the name and telephone number of her friend. "Maybe I should call first," she added.

"Good idea. Will you do it after we eat? Then I can go over to see her this morning." He replaced the notebook and reached for his fork. "We'll be using the Sea Breeze Motel on St. Simons for the people coming in from Washington. That's where you'll be working. The coffee shop will be the press room."

"Do you mean that you make all the arrangements for the national press, too?" She paused with a forkful of eggs halfway to her mouth. "Who pays for all this?" she asked.

He reached for a slice of toast and spread it liberally with her mother's homemade strawberry preserves. "It's safer and more convenient for us to manage the preparations. We organize their travel, set up the press room, make their reservations and then send a bill to their networks or publishers."

Miranda pondered this information while they ate. Her idea of a Secret Service agent's job was to stand next to the president when he was in public and to protect him from harm. She'd had no inkling of the work that went on behind the scenes.

Jake gave a gratified sigh and put down his cup. "That was delicious. I'd like to spend the day right here with you." He let his gaze wander over the scene before him. "Sand, sea and sunshine," he added wistfully before his eyes returned to her. "And a beautiful woman."

Miranda returned his smile. "I can see where I rate," she teased.

"You know better than that." He rose, circled

the table, and pulled her to her feet. She made no protest when he brought her into a light embrace. "How long have your parents had this place?"

Was there a note of reserve in his voice? "It belonged to my grandfather. When I was little we'd come here as soon as school was out for the summer. Daddy commuted on weekends. It always made me sad when we had to leave again."

"It sounds like you had a very happy childhood." He tugged lightly on her hair to tip her face up.

"I did." She searched his features. The dark eyes were unrevealing until they dropped to her lips. She held her breath as he lowered his head. Her lashes dropped and her sigh was lost in his mouth. But the kiss was over too soon.

"I've got to earn my salary," he muttered huskily, setting her away from him. "Will you call your friend?"

A few minutes later they were in the study, a comfortable, book-lined room that Jake barely glanced at. He was watching Miranda's lips as she explained the reason for her call.

She had the sweetest mouth. Fascinated, he studied the white even teeth, the tip of her tongue, the full lower lip and the sensuous arch of the upper. He could spend a lot of time exploring that soft warm cavern, he decided. Her mouth was expressive in conversation. She smiled at something her friend said and her lips stretched taut. He was drawn as though on a string toward that honeyed moistness. Forcibly he jerked his head back, spinning on his heel to examine the closest shelf of books and plunged his hands into the pockets of his jeans.

Why had he hesitated when she offered herself as a local volunteer? She was certainly familiar with the area, and her parents were now permanent residents. She'd be perfectly qualified. But he'd felt a definite reluctance to involve her, when what he should be feeling was gratitude that one more detail was taken care of.

Miranda, like any other woman in whom he'd had a personal interest, belonged in another compartment of his life, separated from his job completely. That was how he managed his relationships so well. Why had he even mentioned the need for a volunteer? He could easily have asked someone else for suggestions. He should have known that Miranda would offer to do it herself. But it was too late now.

He probably would have had no hesitation at all if she hadn't brought up the subject of danger. Most of the time this was a routine job, and he had a tendency to forget the dangerous moments. Crazies and weirdos were a fact of life, usually more talk than threat. But fanatics, of whom there seemed to be a growing number every day, were a real danger. And any reminder of danger was a reminder of Harry, his mentor and teacher, who had been killed in the line of duty four years ago by just such a fanatic. And of Harry's wife.

PATRICIA SANDERS WAS MIRANDA'S AGE, but to Jake the resemblance ended there. The small brunette was the wife of a doctor and the mother of three children, all under school age. "She needs a break from changing diapers. And her mother, who lives nearby, will take care of the children," Miranda had told him.

When Jake knocked at the door of the neat brick house and it was opened to the cacophony of a toy drum, a whistle, and the screams of an infant, he knew what Miranda meant. But the lovely woman was as unflappable as though she were taking tea in the Queen's garden.

She smiled serenely when he introduced himself. "How do you do, Mr. Stewart? Won't you come in?"

He followed her through the hall into a den of enormous proportions. She halted in the middle of the floor and clapped her hands loudly. "Sandbox time! Ten-shun!" Drum and whistle hit the floor, and two toddlers, a boy and a girl, stood like tiny soldiers. The wail of the infant was cut off in midscream.

Patricia Sanders lifted the baby from the floor and placed him in a swing in front of the sliding glass door. She swung a crank, and the swing began to rock gently to the tune of "Hush, Little Baby." Then she slid back the glass. Without a word the little soldiers marched through, across the patio and down one step to the lawn. Then their discipline broke, and they squealed and went running toward the sandbox.

The diminutive brunette woman turned back

toward him with a mischievous smile. "They're at the chimpanzee stage."

At his blank look, she giggled. "Easily pro-grammable."

Jake gave a hoot of laughter. He was going to like Miranda's friend.

She bent to place a soft kiss on the head of the somnolent baby. "Come on. We'll go into the kitchen," she whispered and walked him through a jumble of toys spread from wall to wall across the beautifully decorated den.

"The children are rather noisy today," she said placidly as she poured him a cup of coffee.

"I imagine three children their ages are quite a handful," he offered, still admiring the way she managed to look so fragile and feminine after that impressive display of loving tyranny.

She shrugged and refilled her own cup from the percolator, then she joined him at the table. Her bright-blue eyes took in every detail of his appearance. "So you are Jake Stewart," she stated speculatively, as though a reputation had preceded his visit.

Jake had heard most of Miranda's end of the conversation. He couldn't remember anything in her introduction that would warrant such a contemplative statement or thorough visual in-ventory. He was definitely on trial for some reason. "Yes, ma'am," he answered politely. "Have we met?"

Patricia laughed. The sound was tinkly and he enjoyed it. "Of course not. There was just something in Miranda's voice...something I haven't heard for a long time." She lowered her voice to a conspiratorial murmur. "Are you having an affair with Miranda?"

Jake almost choked on his coffee. "No!"

Lifting her cup to her lips she glanced at him sharply. "Would you like to?" she asked.

He shook his head in disbelief, put down his cup and faced the woman squarely. "Are you psychic?" he asked with a gentle half smile.

This time her laughter was undeniably filled with delight. "Good! Miranda has been uptight lately. She needs to have an affair, and I think you'll do just fine. You're very handsome, but in a rugged sort of honest way. Charles was too slick." She dismissed Charles Springer with a wave of her dainty hand.

Jake didn't try to hide his amusement. "I'm glad you approve." A thought struck him, a question he really shouldn't ask. It was none of his business, and the information wasn't vital by the longest stretch of any official's imagination. "Surely there have been men since Charles Springer?"

He tried for nonchalance but Patricia Sanders was anything but dumb. "Are you asking in an official capacity?" she asked cautiously.

He grinned. "No, strictly personal."

"Well, then." She leaned forward like a small bird ready to exchange gossip with the robin on the next branch. Her eyes glistened with interest. "I don't think there has been anyone important. Of course, I can't be sure. She stays in Athens most of the year. But she's never brought anyone home for the holidays. She's very close to her family, and I would think she'd want to introduce them to a man, if he were important to her, wouldn't you?"

He nodded sagely. "I would think so."

"When she's here she dates a lot, but I've never seen her out with the same man more than two or three times." Her eyes widened then narrowed suddenly. "You're not married, are you?" she demanded.

"No," he answered slowly. "My job isn't adaptable to a settled home life."

Again he was subjected to an intense scrutiny. This lady could teach the Secret Service a few things about intimidation, he thought.

"Well, I guess it's for the best," she went on. "I doubt that we could get Miranda to the altar anyway."

Belatedly Jake came to his senses. Miranda would have both their heads if she could overhear their conversation. He could imagine the curses that would rain down on him. And what on earth was happening to him? He *never* behaved unprofessionally. The fact that the president hadn't yet arrived was no excuse; he was not on vacation. He was here to do a job! "Uh . . . Mrs. Sanders."

She smiled prettily. "Patricia, please."

"Patricia," he acknowledged with a brisk nod. "Do you think we could keep this conversation to ourselves?"

Throwing her head, she laughed again with a sound of pure enjoyment. "Oh heavens, yes!"

she said emphatically when she could speak again. "Miranda would kill us! You'd never know it—she's so charming and pleasant—but when she's really angry, Miranda has the most god-awful temper I've ever seen."

"Really?" Jake asked blandly.

"Really." She leaned forward again. "I remember one time...."

IT WAS LATE THAT AFTERNOON before Jake returned to the coach house. He had spent the morning going over the motel to reassure himself that it was adequate for the needs of the press. After lunch at a fast-food place, he met with the installers of the mountains of phone equipment that would be needed.

There was impatience in his step when he passed through the gate in the hedge. He had breakfasted with her this morning, but felt like he hadn't seen her for days. His mind failed to register the fact that he was now thinking of Miranda as "she."

Miranda didn't answer the knock, and she wasn't by the pool. Her car was parked in the courtyard, however, so he circled the house to look for her on the beach. Sure enough, a gaudy umbrella hid her upper body, but he would have known those legs anywhere.

"Have you been out here all day? You'll be burned to a crisp," he observed as he approached.

She lifted the wide straw hat off her face and smiled up at him. "Hi," she greeted him guardedly. "I just came down. Before ten and after four, those are my sunbathing hours in June."

Her hair had been subdued with a clasp at her nape. She wore no makeup, not even a smidgen of lipstick. Her face, what he could see of it, was smeared with lotion, giving it a shiny unadorned look. Large round sunglasses hid her eyes. And she still looked beautiful to him.

The blanket was littered with her accoutrements—sunscreen, paperback novel, a towel and a frosted can of diet cola. He cleared off a spot and sat down beside her, hooking his hands around his knees. "What are your hours in July?" he asked with a grin.

She reached down to smooth the lotion on her leg until it disappeared, absorbed by her skin. It was an unconsciously seductive motion on her part, and an effort on his to keep his hand from following the same path. "By July I'll have a little bit of tan, as much as I'm liable to get with this fair complexion. So I can stay out longer."

His smile faded. By July he would be long gone. He would never see the tan on those gorgeous legs.

"Did you like Patricia?" she asked.

Jake pulled his attention back to her face. "She's nice," he answered absently, squinting his eyes against the sun's glare. "Would you like to go somewhere for dinner?"

Miranda sat up abruptly and reached for the can of cola. The tab came off with a soft hiss,

and she took a long swallow before answering.
"I don't know," she said finally.

"You've been on my mind all day," he admitted quietly. Her lips were moist with the cola and he ached to taste it away.

She ran a finger around the rim of the can, following the motion with her eyes as though it were important.

Finally he could stand her silence no longer. "Miranda, look at me."

She lifted her face, but he couldn't see through the tinted glasses to read her expression. Gently he hooked a forefinger over the crosspiece and pulled them down to the end of her nose. The huge green eyes wore a look of confusion that he couldn't bear. He shoved them back in place and heaved a sigh. "Honey," he said and reached for her free hand.

Her fingers were cool from touching the can and a bit slippery with lotion. He smoothed them between his until the cream disappeared. "Are you afraid of me, Miranda?" Though she didn't move or withdraw her hand, he felt her pulling back behind a barrier he couldn't penetrate.

"No. I'm not afraid of you. I'm only trying to be sensible."

"Don't." What was this cottony feeling in his throat? He raised his gaze. "Don't be sensible."

She was quiet for a long moment. A slow smile stole over her features. "Okay," she agreed.

He blinked at the sudden change in her. "Then you'll have dinner with me?"

"Yes. I'll have dinner with you, take you sightseeing, play Scrabble or checkers or ... or golf. Do you play golf, Jake? We can ride horses on the beach and picnic at the end of the island. Do you play tennis? I'm warning you, I'm very good on the tennis court."

His fingers tightened, stopping the flow of her words. "What you mean is ... we'll get to know each other."

Miranda scrambled to her feet and began gathering up her things. "I knew you were a bright boy," she said as she clapped the wide-brimmed straw hat on her head. "That's exactly what I mean. Would you bring the umbrella, Jake?" she asked over her shoulder, taking his assent for granted. She hurried over the low, grass-spotted dunes toward the house.

Jake watched her sweetly rounded derriere with an appreciative, if grudging, grin. He shook his head, wondering why he adjusted so easily to following her orders. Then he pulled the umbrella stake from the sand and released the catch to close it.

5

FOR THE NEXT THREE DAYS Miranda and Jake spent
every free minute together. He humiliated her
at golf, and she wiped up the tennis court with
him. She won at Scrabble, but he was the better
chess player. They were fairly matched on
horseback, but he was a stronger swimmer and
left her in the middle of the pool on the first lap.

Since Jake's days became more full as the
presidential visit drew nearer, their time together was limited to the late afternoon and
evening hours. It was often after three or later
when he left her to return to the coach house.

Miranda indulged by sleeping in late, but
Jake had to be up at dawn. On the third night,
after they had played nine holes of golf on the
Sea Island course, he fell asleep watching a
movie in her father's study.

She was curled up in a chair when she heard
the soft snoring sound from the figure stretched
out on the leather sofa. She looked across the
remnants of a pizza on the coffee table between
them. Her lips curved in a compassionate smile.

One of his hands was under his head and the
other rested on his flat stomach. They had removed their cleated shoes at the door and his

feet, in dark socks, were crossed at the ankles. His black hair was rumpled endearingly and a lock fell forward over his forehead.

Quietly she got to her feet and circled the table to kneel on the floor beside his shoulder. She studied him for a long time, a luxury she wouldn't allow herself when he was awake.

His features reflected his strength—a firm mouth, determined chin, wide intelligent brow. Tiny lines radiated from the outer corners of his eyes, as though he looked sharply and mindfully at details close at hand and matters far, far away.

Her brows came together in a perplexed frown as she tried to rationalize the fact that she was more drawn to him than she'd ever been to anyone else in her life. At first she tried to tell herself that the attraction was only physical, but as her brow cleared, she finally admitted that some other feeling, some mass or shape melting from around her heart, was tangible evidence that it went far deeper.

She bent her head to place a feather-light kiss on his lips. He stirred and rolled to his side, reaching for her instinctively in his sleep. His arm curved around her shoulders, pulling her face against the abrasive skin of his cheek. He needed a shave. That was odd since she could still smell lingering traces of his after-shave. "Jake," she whispered. "It's time to go home."

"Home?" His murmur was thick but he didn't open his eyes. "I am home."

Very gently Miranda loosened his grasp on

her shoulders and stood looking down at him. He appeared to be comfortable enough. She shrugged and started to reach for the Afghan folded on the back of the sofa, then changed her mind. It wouldn't cover all of him. She left the room and returned a few minutes later with a blanket, which she spread carefully over his long body.

She switched off the television set and the one small lamp that was burning, picked up the big flat pizza box—who would want to wake to the smell of cold pizza?—and tiptoed out of the room.

Two days later Miranda woke up earlier than usual. And for some reason her ex-husband was on her mind, a fact that threatened to ruin her whole day.

Why Charles? She hardly ever thought of him any more unless someone reminded her. The handsome man who had swept her off her feet when she was young had left some scars behind, but they were only surface scars. Their brief marriage had never developed beyond the social arrangement he'd meant it to be.

She crossed her arms behind her head and looked seriously at the ceiling. How bored poor Charles must have been with the adolescent adoration she'd poured out, when all he'd wanted was a wealthy wife with good connections. How deeply had he hurt her? She'd told herself for a long time now that she was better off without him, without any man. But was that true? Charles's bequest to her had been a wariness of getting involved, of letting any man come too close.

Now this damn Yankee had come down and melted the protective shield around her heart, leaving her vulnerable for the first time in her adult life.

She hadn't seen Jake since she had covered him with a blanket that night on the sofa. He had left her a hastily written note explaining that he was going to be very busy for a day or two. But he hadn't even called, and his disregard for her feelings had both hurt and angered her.

Miranda sat straight up in bed. "At least he isn't Charles," she said aloud as she slid off the mattress and padded into the bathroom. Dressing quickly in a pair of white shorts and a lavender halter, she went downstairs.

It was only six-thirty when she took her coffee cup onto the patio and hefted herself up to sit crosslegged on the balustrade. Her gaze wandered across sand that bore no footprints, to the gentle swell of a calm sea. The brightening sky promised a beauutiful day. Even knowing how capricious the weather could be she felt the swell of her customary optimism. The tide smoothed the beach of yesterday's bumps and tracings just as the night soothed the cares of the previous day. Dawn was a new beginning, and she might almost be Eve, Miranda thought quixotically.

Catching movement from the corner of her

eye she swiveled her head to see who else was such an early riser. Viewed from the back, Jake's bronzed body in a bathing suit was a heart-rocking sight. As she watched, the towel draped around his neck was snapped off and dropped carelessly on the beach.

She forgot the hurt and the anger caused by his recent neglect and simply enjoyed the sight of him. Her eyes greedily watched as he jogged across the sand. They traced the broad shoulders and back to where his body narrowed sharply to trim hips and muscular thighs. His long legs carried him toward the water with the agility of a healthy animal.

He had to wade out quite a way before the water was deep enough to dive, but finally he knifed a wave and struck out, his powerful arms surging in a crawl. In minutes he was merely a speck. She held her breath until he turned, heading back to shore.

She wasn't sure when he saw her, but her perch on the balustrade put her above the level of the dunes and well within view of the ocean. When he was about thirty yards out his stroke seemed to hesitate but then immediately picked up rhythm again. He emerged from the waves and strode toward her.

Water streamed from his hair into his face, and he wiped it away. It ran off his shoulders and down his chest, only slightly impeded by the thick growth of hair there. She watched, mesmerized, as he scooped up the towel, slinging it around his neck. By the time he reached the dunes she could see his eyes. Unabashedly she searched his expression, hoping to see some warmth there, but that guarded look was back instead. She sat perfectly still, clutching her fingers together around the coffee cup, hoping he wouldn't hear the thunder that was her heart.

Finally he stood before her, looking for all the world as though he belonged there, as though she had been waiting for him. The realization filled her with sudden embarrassment. Pride dictated that she respond indifferently, and her wonderful temper came to her rescue. Her chin went up a notch. "Good morning."

"I've missed you," he said.

"You managed to hide it well," she answered, not attempting to keep the sarcasm out of her voice. She unfolded her bare legs so they hung on the balustrade.

Jake took a step and placed his hands on either side of her knees. "I was trying to give you time to decide about me, about us."

"Good. I've decided. I want you to leave me alone." Her tone was flat and final.

"I can't do that." He inhaled deeply and audibly, and let his breath out. "Miranda, the morning I woke up on your sofa...do you know what I did?"

"I neither know nor care," she said shortly. "Would you please go away?"

"I came upstairs to watch you sleep," he told her gently.

She caught her breath and looked down at

her coffee. Reflected in its dark surface she saw her own eyes and was shocked at the expression of desire in them.

"I must have sat for an hour in that chair beside your bed. I wanted you so much."

A sob lodged in her throat briefly before breaking free. "You could have called," she said huskily, revealing the depth of her hurt.

"If I'd heard your voice, if we'd been together, there would have been no way in hell I could have kept from making love to you."

The statement drew her gaze to his brown eyes, and, once he had her complete attention, he held it deliberately. He went on in a tone laced with unmistakable sincerity. "Miranda, we can't ignore each other, and we can't be merely friends. I tried both and it won't work. Not for me anyway."

Her green eyes darkened to jade. She moistened her lips, then realizing what she'd done she wrenched her gaze away and looked out over the ocean.

But he was too near. It was impossible not to look at him, not to be totally aware of his lips, inches from hers. Without thinking—she wasn't capable of thought—she leaned forward and touched his lips lightly with hers. His mouth was cool and tasted of the sea.

His eyes flared at the action, and he smiled . . . a lazy smile that slashed the furrow in his cheek, but he didn't move.

Reluctantly she returned the smile. "I have a horrible premonition that you're right." She emptied the cold coffee out onto the sand, swung her legs around and dropped to the terrace, leaving the balustrade between them.

Jake grasped the ends of his towel. The movement was calculated to be casual but she noticed that his knuckles were white. He was as unsure as she was. The knowledge made her feel better.

"I have some steaks in the freezer," she said finally with a sigh of resignation.

"What time?" he asked immediately.

"Seven," she answered. "But this doesn't mean...."

He leaned across the wall between them to take hold of her shoulders. Pulling her forward he covered her lips with a quick kiss. "I know what it doesn't mean," he said tenderly. "See you at seven."

She watched him go, knowing that she had capitulated. At least she hadn't mentioned how much she had missed him. The past two days might have been a month. Despite her uneasiness, she knew exactly what was going to happen that night and she was scared.

JAKE APPEARED AT THE KITCHEN DOOR on the dot of seven. His jeans had been discarded in favor of a pair of well-tailored gray slacks, a light-blue shirt open at the throat, and a hand-tailored navy blazer. He smelled of spicy after-shave and looked so fresh and appealing that Miranda almost dropped the bottle of wine he handed her. She was glad that she had decided to wear a sun dress, however casual.

He eyed her bare shoulders with an appreciative look. "I thought redheads weren't supposed to wear pink but you are lovely in that color," he told her huskily.

"Thank you." Miranda took a step backwards and to the side and clutched the bottle to her middle with both hands. "Come in."

Jake took a few steps into the kitchen and turned to smile—that warm sexy smile that had such a powerful effect. She met his smile with a steady one of her own, praying he was unaware of what her poise cost her. "What will you have to drink?" she asked steadily.

Jake opened the button of the blazer and slid his hands into the pockets of his trousers. "Scotch, if you have it. Can I help?"

His mood was certainly light, in contrast to hers, she thought grumpily. Ever since he'd left her on the beach she'd felt the tension forming knotted ribbons inside her, re-forming into restless butterflies now that he was actually here. She swallowed hard. "No. You go out onto the patio. I'll be along in just a minute."

He disappeared through the door to the hall without argument, and she breathed a sigh of relief. This wasn't a good idea. She was so aware of his masculine appeal that her pulse was never stable when she was in his presence. If she escaped from this relationship unscathed it would be a miracle.

Five minutes later she nudged the French door open with the toe of her high-heeled sandal, a silver tray in her hands.

Jake stood with one forearm on the balustrade, the other hand jingling the change in his pocket. He straightened immediately. "Let me take that." He relieved her of the tray and set it on the same round table they had breakfasted on. Only now the table was covered with a white damask cloth. Candles, protected from the breeze by hurricane shades, waited to be lit when the sun disappeared completely, and there were places laid for two with silver, china and crystal.

Miranda had replaced the brightly colored cushions on the wrought-iron furniture. She looked around in dismay. Would he think she had set the scene to impress him? Hastily she picked up both glasses and handed him the one containing Scotch. "This is yours."

His mouth curved up on one side. "I gathered," he said evenly.

She took a hasty sip from the ruby liquid in her glass. "This is very good. Thank you for bringing it."

"I'm glad you like it." His deep male dimple winked at her.

"Shall we sit down?" she offered formally.

Instead he gave a sigh of resigned amusement. He shook his head, his mouth curving in that devastating smile, and took the glass from her unsteady fingers. "Miranda," he scolded gently as he placed both glasses on the low wall. "Don't look at me as though I were the hangman."

She bit back a hysterical laugh. "I'm not," she denied without much sincerity.

"Oh, hell!" he said exasperatedly. "Let's get this over with."

"Get what over with?"

"This first kiss. Then maybe you'll relax." He reached for her unresisting body and brought her into his arms with a determined move. He didn't kiss her at once, but held her against his tall form, looking deeply into her eyes. "You are as nervous as a cat, sweetheart. Calm down."

"Oh, for heaven's sake, Jake. I'm not a child and I am calm," she informed him shortly. But the warmth from his body was seeping into her limbs, turning them to jelly.

"You needn't be afraid either. I told you, I won't do anything you don't want me to do."

She relaxed all of a sudden, tucking her head under his jaw, like the helpless child she'd denied being, seeking solace. His arms felt so good, so right around her like this. He had read her mood precisely. She was nervously waiting for him to pounce. "That's the point, Jake, I do want you to make love to me."

He chuckled, the sound warm and welcome under her cheek, and his arms tightened. "Thank God," he murmured unsteadily against her temple. "That's quite an admission, sweetheart. I don't think I could have stood it if you'd turned me away tonight."

"I've thought about it a lot. It's not a spur-of-the-moment decision." She didn't want him to get the wrong impression, she told herself. Then she pulled that thought back sharply. What did she care what kind of impression he got? This wasn't going to be a lasting relationship.

She could feel the tremor in his hand as he stroked the mane of her hair. "It's been a long time for you, hasn't it, honey?"

She lifted her head, about to admit the truth of his statement, when a horrible thought struck her. "What did you and Patricia talk about the other day?" she challenged abruptly, the light of battle in her eyes.

He covered her lips with his in a kiss of such hunger, such explosive warmth, that Miranda completely forgot her question. His tongue probed greedily, urging her to respond, and she let her lashes drift down protectively against the blaze in his eyes, giving herself up to pure sensation.

The circle of his arms became like heated bands of iron, and she slid her hands under his jacket, flattening her palms over the rippling muscles in his back in an attempt to fuse their bodies together. Curves melted against hard angular planes. He pulled his mouth away for a millisecond to fill his lungs, and then the onslaught began anew.

But Miranda needed air, too, and when a whimper signaling that need escaped from her throat he finally seemed to recall himself. His arms loosened a fraction, and he diverted his mouth to the tiny pulse racing wildly at the base of her throat. "Have you put the steaks on yet?" he demanded hoarsely.

She shook her head in protest of such a mun-

dane question at a time like this. One large hand
tangled in her hair as he lifted his head to con-
tinue the magic of his kisses over her cheeks,
her closed eyes, the arch of her brows. His
breath on her skin was warm and sweet. "Have
you?" he repeated.

"No." The word was merely a sigh, but he
heard.

"Then we're going to have a very late dinner."
He stated, propeling her toward the French
doors. When they were inside he turned away
from her briefly to lock them.

Miranda's knees refused to sustain her weight,
and she leaned against the wall, watching as he
fumbled with the brass handles. Her lips curved
in a smile at the soft expletive he uttered.

The lock shot home. He turned to her and
paused. His eyes narrowed, then focused on the
green fire in hers. He approached slowly, bringing his lower body in alignment with her hips,
pinning her effectively against the wall. Had it
not been for the tender yearning in his expression she would have protested the dominating
maneuver, but in her dazed state she found it
very sensual.

His hands came up to cup the fullness of her
breasts through the soft fabric. "Why are you
smiling that sly little smile?" he asked, his voice
low and melodious.

She caught her breath at the sharp pleasure of
his touch, and then his hands were reaching behind her for the zipper of the dress. Cool air

struck her skin as he carefully peeled the top down to her waist. Still he didn't release her gaze. Instinct and experience led his hands to the catch of her strapless bra, and it was disposed of quickly. "You haven't answered my question," he murmured silkily.

"I...oh!" She gasped when the heels of his hands took the weight of her breasts, the slightly calloused pads of his fingers stroked across her nipples.

He bent his head to tease one corner of her mouth with his tongue, breaking, at last, the mastery of his gaze. "Yes?" he whispered encouragingly.

The word barely registered above the muffled thud of her heartbeat. Her head fell back against the wall. Desire, a scorching, fervid desire, had invaded her body, leading her into the full confidence of anticipation, sweeping away any remnant of hesitancy. "I-I was just wondering whether or—" she stopped to swallow "—whether or not we'd make it to my bedroom."

He chuckled into her mouth. "Most definitely." With a smooth, swift move he picked her up and headed toward the staircase. "I want everything to be perfect for you, honey. And as romantic as it may sound to get so carried away that you make love on the floor, it isn't very comfortable."

He shifted her in his arms, baring her thigh, and his fingers seemed to burn there as he climbed the steps. Miranda wrapped her arms around his neck and clung, sprinkling small kisses along his jaw line. "Is this part of the advance planning you told me about?"

He had just put his foot down on the top step, but at her words he froze. All the color drained from his face. "Oh, hell! Advance planning." The phrase was ripped from him. His arms tightened possessively, his fingers biting into her thigh. "Miranda, dammit! I didn't *do* any advance planning!"

She almost laughed aloud at the look of total dismay on his face. His brows rose in the middle and his mouth drooped at the corners. He looked like a small boy who had been told he would have to skip Christmas this year.

One rosy-tipped finger traced the dark brows, erasing the dismal expression and her palm cradled his cheek. "Poor baby," she clucked consolingly, but her eyes were bright with a wicked gleam.

"Miranda! You don't understand."

"Don't worry. I did my own advance planning," she said, smiling softly.

His brow cleared. "You did?"

Her calm "Yep" brought forth a whoop of delighted relief, and they both dissolved into laughter as he carried her in to dump her without ceremony on her bed. "Miranda, you are a woman in a million," he said as he strode briskly from window to window lowering the shades.

Miranda plumped up the pillows behind her and settled back to watch. His jacket hit the floor lamp; his shirt, the edge of a chair. He used his toes to loosen the loafers and kicked them away impatiently while he unbuckled his belt.

His legs were tanned and sinewy and heavily sprinkled with hair. The briefs did nothing to hide his arousal. "You're overdressed," he murmured as he approached the bed.

Miranda's dress was still half off, but she had been too enthralled with the sight of his masculine figure to notice. Suddenly she felt shy. She reached for the bodice of her dress.

His hands were there to stop her. "No, my lovely redheaded sorceress," he rasped hoarsely. "Don't hide from me."

The haste that had compelled him seemed to dissolve with his words. His hands closed firmly on her shoulders but their touch was slow and lingering, not impatient.

Lifting her to her knees on the edge of the bed, he tugged the dress over her head and tossed it aside, while his eyes drifted leisurely over her. Carefully his arms drew her forward, bringing her breasts into tender contact with his chest. The friction there was exciting, stimulating against her sensitive nipples.

He wrapped the long swathe of her copper-colored hair around his fist and bent his head to plant heated kisses at her nape. The sensations of warmth and desire radiated throughout her body, filling her with voluptuous yearning. She murmured something incoherent even to herself.

His fingers slip down her body and beneath an elastic barrier to define her rounded bottom with a languid caress, then he removed the lace bikini panties. Gently he urged her back until she sat with her legs curled beneath her. He stood for a long moment drinking in his fill of her.

She was equally curious and allowed her gaze to drift over him. By the time her eyes returned to his face her lids were heavy with passion. "Jake," she whispered weakly.

That was all—just his name, but it produced a flare in his eyes. "You have the body of a goddess," he said hoarsely.

The blood in her veins rushed to nourish the sensitive nerves near the surface of her skin, resulting in a delightful blush, all over. He smiled at the sight, putting out a long finger to stroke the rosy color at her throat.

When he joined her on the bed, it was to enfold her at once in a tender yet hungry embrace, his hands soothing on her back, her shoulders, her arms. One hair-roughened leg hooked over her thighs, bringing her close into the force of his arousal. "I want to kiss every velvet inch of you," he whispered at her ear. His tongue drew an arc around its curve and his teeth closed on the lobe.

Miranda buried her eager hands in the dark thickness of his hair, reveling in tactile delight as she combed the strands with her fingers. Her hips moved unguardedly in response to his promise.

A groan escaped from deep within his chest. At the same time his breathing rate increased. He twisted her to her back and, supporting himself on his forearms, began his sensual journey at her white breasts. His palms flattened at the outer curves while his lips explored the cleavage he'd made. Turning his face against her he sought the hard peaks, circling them, wetting them with his tongue. His mouth opened over the tender points to suckle and tease, kiss and blow gently, until Miranda was twisting hungrily beneath him.

His hands slid slowly down her body as his mouth continued its sweet torment. He whispered words of praise as he found places she had never known were sensitive to erotic stimulation, the curve of her waist, the backs of her knees, the high arch of her foot. At last he slid his hands beneath her hips, lifting her into the most erotic experience of all. She couldn't control the desperate little whimper that broke from her lips.

With gentle pressure and passionate grace he melded two into one. Miranda felt tears sting her eyes at the beauty of his caring completion. "Oh, Jake," she whispered.

Then, caught in the rhythm of his movement, his virile thrust, she knew no more than the cloud of stardust surrounding their joined bodies. It muffled the sounds of their breathing, wrapping them in a misty veil, expanding like a heavenly fog until suddenly the firmament burst apart with all the dynamism of a nova explosion. She clung to him against the power and energy that threatened to sweep away her consciousness.

When she could open her eyes again she looked up at him, awed with the miracle of the experience, and saw her wonder reflected in his burning gaze. She had to close her eyes against its brilliance. He sealed them shut with tender kisses and started to roll away from her, but she tightened her arms. "No, please," she begged in whisper. She didn't want to lose him, not yet.

"Aren't I too heavy, sweetheart?" he asked softly.

She shook her head. Never too heavy, never.

6

JAKE WAS PROPPED against the pillow-cushioned headboard. He tucked his chin to his chest, regarding the head that rested so comfortably over his heart. Flame hair spread across her shoulders and between his fingers. The strands spilled over his arm, which curved protectively around her, and down her back to make a vivid splash on the white sheet. Why did his skin seem so warm wherever the brilliant curls lay?

For the first time in many years he found himself wondering if he had pleased a woman. He hadn't had any doubts on that score since his adolescent years, he thought wryly, so what was it about Miranda that made him feel anxious, uncertain?

She had most definitely pleased him. She was sweetly captivating, needing only a bit of encouragement, of reassurance, to bring the fabulous self-confidence of her public person to an equally spirited and confident lover. He remembered her absolute delight as he discovered unexpected places on her body that responded erotically to his caress. What a fool her husband must have been. This woman was born to love.

Love? His thoughts came to a sudden halt.

He adjusted their direction. This woman was born to be a lover.

Satisfied at the correction of a minor detail, he resumed his reflections. Her sensuality was as ingrained as her temper, he mused, and needed just as light a provocation to bring it forth.

Suddenly he knit his brows in a frown. His mind was trained to be instinctively alert to danger, and at the image of Miranda's sensuality, a caution light came on.

He tried to dismiss the warning. Yet it was with some misgiving and a strange feeling of sadness that he allowed his eyes to roam slowly over their entwined bodies. They fit together too well. Her legs were almost as long as his, he noted as his gaze traveled up their length, and beautifully shaped. Her calves were firm and strong, and her thighs...oh Lord, her thighs were soft. Firmly he removed his gaze from her thighs.

Her hand rested lightly palm down on his stomach, her thumb and first three fingers on the tanned portion, and the little finger extended in a decidedly feminine position, as though she were holding a teacup, on the skin that seldom saw the sun. He remembered how passionately those hands had explored his own body.

While he watched, the slender digit moved in an absent way, stroking. The muscles under her hand contracted violently, and he sat up so abruptly that her head bounced off his chest.

"How about those steaks?" he said heartily. "Aren't you hungry?"

With a bewildered smile she looked up from where he had dumped her.

Before she could answer he had rolled off the bed and was reaching for his pants. "If you don't mind, I'll make use of your shower." Don't worry that I'll use all—or any—of the *hot* water, he added silently, and disappeared into the bathroom.

Miranda stared blankly at the door, which had been closed with a "stay out" sort of a snap. Then she shrugged and stretched languidly against the pillow, a contented smile shaping her swollen lips. She supposed that, if he were hungry, she would have to feed him. A devilish gleam in her eyes turned the smile into a full-blown grin. Food first, then she would see to his other appetites.

She used the guestroom bath. Twisting her hair into a topknot, she anchored it with a comb. Her shower was leisurely. She opted for the use of a fine imported sponge rather than the invigorating stimulation of a washcloth. The lovely lethargy was the aftermath of their loving and she didn't want to lose it.

When she returned to her bedroom, wrapped in a thick towel, she could still hear the water running. On impulse she crossed to where he had thrown his shirt and picked it up, sliding her arms into the sleeves. It smelled of him. She dropped the towel, and, wrapping the shirt around her, stepped to the mirror. Not bad. The tails covered her nicely, front and back, and the curved hem on the sides was just the slightest bit provocative. As she finished fastening the last button, the sound of the water stopped.

"Miranda?" Jake stuck his head out of the bathroom and looked around the empty bedroom. With a sigh of relief he came out, wearing his wrinkled pants.

Her brush was on the dresser. He borrowed it to smooth his rumpled hair. The mirror was low, so he bent his knees and tilted his body to see what he was doing. Under his upraised arms he met his own eyes in the mirror. The cold shower had helped, for now, but the guarded expression that was habitual with him had softened, giving his features an exposed cast that he wasn't at all comfortable with.

He threw the brush down in disgust. Emotionalism of any type was foreign to him, unwanted and inappropriate. Taking a woman to bed was a pleasant pastime, physically and mentally satisfying, but he had never risen from bed with this unsettled feeling before. Deliberately he tightened his jaw and looked around for the rest of his clothes.

When Jake entered the kitchen Miranda was humming softly to herself. Potatoes were in the microwave and the salad had been made before he arrived. She'd arranged two steaks on a broiling pan and sprinkled them with ground pepper. Now she was crushing oregano between her palms, warming it to release the bouquet. She held her hands over the steaks, directing the dusting of spice to their surface carefully.

He jammed his hands into his pockets and glowered at her long legs. "Can I help?" he asked harshly.

The sound of his voice startled her and she jumped. She swung around, powdering the floor with oregano, and gave him her warmest smile. "You can keep me company," she offered.

The morning they had cooked breakfast together she'd done her best to avoid touching him. Now she wanted him to come closer, to enfold her in his arms, to let her face rest on his bare chest.

But he stayed where he was, just inside the door, and his expression was grim.

The intensity of her disappointment shocked her. What had happened to put that withdrawal on his face? Had she done something? She swallowed, returning her attention to the steaks, blinking furiously against the hot sting behind here eyes. He had shown her a crack in the door to another world, a glorious world to be explored with him. Was he closing it in her face? Well, she refused to be shut out.

With a definite swipe she rid her palms of oregano flakes and opened the oven to slide the pan under the hot broiler. Then she turned to face him, her hands balled in fists and planted on her hips. "What's the matter?" she snapped.

He didn't know what made him snap back at

her. Perhaps it was the sight of her in his shirt, which provoked a growing arousal he couldn't control. "I've just spent thirty minutes in a damn cold shower! That's what's the matter. Then I come down here to find you dressed like the centerfold in *Playboy* in *my* shirt!"

Her knees threatened to give way at first, and her heart gave a leap. A cold shower? He was barricading himself as though she were a threat. Nonsense. She was no threat to anyone, she thought in confusion. But his resentment shone clearly in his eyes, in the defensive posture of his body.

At last her temper came to her rescue. With a proud tilt to her chin she jerked at the buttons of the offending garment. With furious ease considering how her fingers had trembled while trying to get them fastened, they parted. She slid the shirt off her shoulders and threw it at him. "Here! I apologize! I didn't realize it was hallowed property!"

Naked as the day she was born, she stepped past him, her chin still firm, taking unholy pleasure in his stunned expression.

"Miranda, wait. . . ." The shirt fell unnoticed to the floor.

She slapped at the hand that reached out to detain her, but he was only diverted for the blink of an eye. His next try was more successful. He swung her around and into his arms. "Stop it," he commanded.

"I don't take orders, Mr. Secret Service Man." She squirmed in an effort to free herself, but it was the wrong thing to do. She felt his instant response.

Jake groaned and covered her mouth in a desperate kiss. His arms tightened convulsively. "Please, stop it," he implored against her lips. "I'm sorry. It's just that...I can't...." He mouthed his way over her face hungrily to bury his face in her neck. His words were almost incoherent. "Miranda...love...I'm not usually so out of control."

She quieted in his arms. Tentatively she wrapped her own arms around his waist, careful not to hold on too tight. "And you don't like being out of control," she said in a low voice. It explained a lot.

"It scares the hell out of me," he admitted huskily.

His words were quite a confession. She wasn't sure that even he knew how much of a confession they were. Her insight led her to finish his unspoken thought. The attraction between them was too strong for him to be comfortable in a relationship with her. What was she supposed to do about that? Blinking at the ceiling, she willed calmness into her voice. "Jake, let me go put on some clothes," she requested reasonably.

He raised his head. For a long moment they looked at each other. Then he shook his head. "Hell, no." He released her and reached down for his shirt, holding it open for her.

She hesitated only for a moment, searching his eyes, before turning to slip her arms back into the sleeves. His fingers were deft and purposeful as he buttoned it again, but his voice held the slightest tremor as he asked, "Now, can't I help with something?"

"You can light the candles and fix us fresh drinks, if you like," she answered softly. "Everything else is ready."

He drew her gently into his arms. She felt his lips against her forehead. They stood quietly, in benign contrast to all earlier embraces, drawing strength from each other, until the aroma of the broiling meat awakened their other senses.

"Don't you dare burn my steak, woman," Jake mumbled affectionately and rumpled her hair.

If his hand trembled just a bit as it lingered at her crown, she chose not to comment, because she was trembling, too. "Do you like it rare?" she asked, pulling out of his arms to hurry to the stove.

"Almost raw," he declared with a grin.

She shook her head in mock resignation. "I should have known. It's probably the animal in you."

"Definitely," he growled. "And a hungry animal is dangerous."

How well I know, she agreed to herself.

THE CANDLES WERE FLICKERING ANXIOUSLY, consuming the last bit of wax in their holders. The light from the waning moon gave only weak illumination to the scene, relegating the house behind them to the shadows of the night, and reminding Miranda of the evening they'd met. That night the moon had washed them with a brighter, fuller glow. And like the moon their hours together were wasting away, with the same inevitability.

In the isolated glimmer of the candles the more subtle nuances of their expressions were unreadable, but the dialogue throughout dinner had been disquietingly light.

Jake sat back in his chair with a sigh of repletion and put down his fork. "That is the most delicious pie I've ever tasted. What do you call it?"

Miranda gave him a teasing smile over her last bite. When the concoction of ice cream, chocolate, and meringue had melted away on her tongue she answered, "It's called a 'Girdle Buster.'"

His laugh was unrestrained. "Appropriate, if unromantic. But in this shirt, it could be dangerous."

She had found a clean sweatshirt of her father's in the laundry room for him. The material was stretched to its limit, threatening the seams, but he looked magnificent in it.

Reaching for his wineglass he toasted her. "The entire meal was delicious. Including the hors d'oeuvre," he added in a low voice, barely audible over the sound of the waves.

Suddenly one of the candles gave a last bright gasp before it died. In the unexpected illumination she saw the sadness mingled with desire in his eyes.

She shook off an unwelcome sense of forboding and stood. "I'd like to walk on the beach."

"Lead the way," he agreed lightly.

Jake watched as Miranda buried her toes in the sand. The breeze was slight but enough to tease him with the sight of his shirt molding itself lovingly to the full, upthrusting curves of her breasts, the hem playing against her thighs. The faint moonlight dusted her face with silver and turned her russet hair almost black.

Suddenly she laughed. Holding her arms out from her body she danced across the sand to dip her feet in the water.

She's like a sprite, a nymph, thought Jake, *a bewitching enchantress*. He watched, thoroughly bemused by the sight, while a strange feeling crept over him, a feeling that she might take wing and sail into the star-studded sky. An overwhelming urge to catch her in his arms, to hold her to the ground, gripped him.

He shoved his hands into the pockets of his slacks. Damn! He was drawn to her like a magnet, but he must—had to—break this field of force.

Breathless she came back to him, holding out her hand. "Isn't it wonderful?" she cried exuberantly.

He could no more have resisted her enthusiasm than he could a tidal wave. He took her hand and followed her over the sand. The radiance that warmed her from within spilled over, drenching him in a pleasure like none he'd ever known.

Inhaling the perfume from her hair, he closed

his eyes to mask the sharp thrust of emotion he felt, an unfamiliar and frightening emotion that was more than desire, so much more.

"I've got to be going," he said suddenly. *Yes! Go. Get away from here.* The caution light had turned from yellow to red, flashing its danger sign. *Leave, before you get so mired in a relationship you can't extricate yourself.* He hadn't realized how coldly his words had come out until he saw the hurt and confusion in Miranda's eyes. The accusation there, too, was deserved. He had convinced her to admit the feelings between them, to surrender to those feelings, and now he was denying them himself.

Her withdrawal was quick and complete. She dropped his hand and turned toward the house. The deep sense of loss and guilt that swamped him was a shock to his system. His heart felt as though it was being squeezed by a giant hand.

With his long legs he was beside her in only two strides, but he didn't try to touch her. "Miranda, let me explain."

"There's nothing to explain. We had a pleasant tumble in the hay and now it's over."

"It wasn't like that and you know it!" he said in exasperation. He wasn't handling this well.

She whirled on him, the tears in her eyes blindingly bright even in the faint light. "Then explain!" she demanded. "But do a better job than you did in the kitchen! I could have saved a darn good steak if I hadn't been so blind."

His sigh was really more of a shudder. "Look, let's go inside ... sit down—"

"No, we can sit right here." She plunked herself in the sand and crossed her legs. Her words and phrases spoke of indifference and independence but her body language said something different. Her arms were folded protectively across her midriff.

He hunkered down in front of her, his hands dangling between his knees. "Miranda, I don't want to hurt you," he said quietly. But he had. He had wounded this beautiful, sensitive woman, whom he wanted . . . and didn't want to want. He was filled with self-loathing.

"What makes you so sure you could?" she demanded, but he heard the tremor in her voice. "I don't allow myself to be hurt by egotistical, self-centered men."

"I won't try to deny that what we have is very special, like nothing I've ever felt for a woman." She was silent. "But marriage is not in my plans," he blurted.

She hooked a strand of hair behind her ear and gave a nervous laugh. "You talk like I'm just waiting to snare you. Did it ever occur to you that I might not be looking for a husband?"

"At the risk of sounding conceited, no. You would eventually begin thinking along those lines, Miranda. You're the kind of woman that a man ends up marrying despite himself."

She met his eyes then. He tried to keep his features expressionless.

"You—you care for me?" she whispered.

He answered ambiguously. "It would never work. Our lives are so totally different that there would be no way to mesh them. No way at all. It's better to stop it now.''

Miranda searched his features for something, anything, to explain why he was doing this. ''Our backgrounds *are* different,'' she said slowly. ''I can't help the fact that my parents are wealthy. But give me credit, I don't live like this in Athens, Jake. My life-style is very simple.''

Her misconception was merely a way out, a means of escape, and he took it without hesitation but with a feeling of guilt. Still it was better for her to think that the problems were compounded by her wealth. She wouldn't understand his unwavering conviction that a Secret Service agent should not be married, and he would never change his mind on that score.

''It wouldn't work, Miranda,'' he repeated. ''You are a part of all this.'' He indicated the beach and its environs with a sweep of his hand. ''Sea Island is really your home. You grew up in a cradle of total security. There is no way I could offer you anything comparable.''

She turned her head away as though she couldn't bear to look at him. This time her laugh was bitter. ''You don't know me at all, Jake. You may think you do, but you don't.'' Slowly she unwound her legs and got to her feet. ''If I've gotten under your skin, I apologize. But you're not giving me an opportunity to prove myself.'' Despite the weight of sadness on her heart she heard what she was saying and was embarrassed at the pleading note in her words.

He straightened, too, even more slowly. Her shoulders drew back, and her chin took on that proud angle that made him want to kiss her senseless. His hands, in his pockets, curled into tight fists in order to fight the urge.

"I'll admit that I was attracted to you, more than I've ever been—" Her voice broke, but not her dignity. She looked him squarely in the eye. "I thought you were adaptable to any situation. But, believe it or not, I *can* live without you." She finished with a defiant toss of her head and left him standing there, while she made her way confidently over the dunes to the house.

Jake stood on the empty beach for a long time. He had made up his mind many years ago that the Service was no life for a married man. He had seen too many marriages go sour because of the extended time spent apart, the complete loyalty demanded outside the marriage. No woman was strong enough, he'd told himself. True, there were some good marriages, but they were the exception rather than the rule. Even the ones that worked were rocky on occasion.

And when children came along...well, he knew that he didn't want children who might have to grow up with a part-time father, or with no father at all. The danger inherent in his job wasn't something he dwelled on, but it was a fact.

He thought of the scar under his arm, the scar that Miranda had traced with a finger, but not inquired about. He thought again of Harry, as he had so often over the past few days . . . Harry who had been killed in the line of duty. Whose wife had made his life a living hell, and who, by her own hand, had finally joined him in death. It was no life for a woman.

As he turned toward the Webster's house he automatically scanned the area as he was trained to do. But the beach was empty. He was alone. And that was the way he wanted it. That was the way it *had* to be, dammit!

7

THE ENERGY WAS TANGIBLE in room 103, the largest of the guest rooms at the Sea Breeze Motel. The regular furniture had been moved out to make space for tables, filing cabinets, computer terminals and banks of telephones.

Two men were leaving as Miranda approached the open door. Their eyes, which at first seemed only mildly curious, took in every minute detail of her appearance: the flaming hair, which had been subdued in a proper bun at her nape, the conservative yellow tailored blouse and dark-green skirt, the fact that she wore no jewelry. When they finished their perusal she was convinced that both of them would recognize her ten years from now, even if she were floating down the Nile in harem pants. She was getting used to being observed so closely.

Patricia was already looking slightly harassed. "I thought Jake said this job was a breeze," she complained happily as she reached her hand out at the shrill demand of a phone.

There was a grunt from the man seated at the computer with his back to the door, but he didn't turn.

"Yes?" Patricia put the phone to her ear and made a face at Miranda. "Yes, ma'am, I understand. You didn't see the notice that came out over the wire." She picked up a pencil and began writing. "Of course we can arrange for press clearance. If you'll just give me your name, date of birth, social security number and the name of your publication ... sorry, my mistake, the call letters of your station." She paused. "Yes, ma'am. You can pick up your credentials here anytime before the president's arrival."

Miranda was aware of Jake even before he spoke from the doorway behind her, but she didn't turn. She wasn't ready to face him, not with the ravages of a sleepless night evident in her eyes.

"Good morning, Miranda." His voice was businesslike. "Barney, will you show Miss Woodbarry the procedure?"

The rather slight man swung his chair around on its rollers and got to his feet, giving Jake a rueful grin. "Sorry, Miss Woodbarry. I didn't hear you come in."

He was a pleasant enough looking man. Average coloring, average size, but there was nothing average about the intelligence in his gray gaze. It was shrewd, astute, with the same qualities of penetration she'd noticed in the other agents. She returned his smile, feeling slightly daunted. "That's okay. And my name is Miranda."

Another phone began to ring, and Jake reached

from behind her to pick it up. Her withdrawal
was automatic, the action she would take if her
hand were too near a hot stove. She didn't even
realize that she'd shrunk aside until she saw the
quizzical look on Barney's face, and felt the
stiffening in Jake's large frame. Luckily, Patricia was concentrating on her phone call.

Barney swung a table aside to let her into the
room, and that was when she realized the furniture was arranged to protect the filing cabinets and the computers. Anyone who wandered
in would have difficult access.

He began to explain the rather simple procedure to her, and Miranda tried desperately to
focus her attention on his words. But it was difficult not to be aware of the man on the phone.
She risked a glance. Jake was bent at the waist,
the phone cradled against his cheek, one broad
hand steadying the pad on which he wrote.
"Yes, sir. If you'd like to call back in about an
hour I can have that information for you," he
was saying. The voice was as smooth and
strong as the line of his body leaning over the
table, and equally exciting.

One leg was slightly bent, increasing the
pressure of denim over a masculine thigh. His
wrists and forearms were tanned and sinewy.
Just above the elbow his muscles thickened,
straining the sleeve of his burgundy knit shirt.
Hooked to his belt was what she presumed to
be some kind of walkie-talkie. She had never
seen him wear it before.

Miranda took a breath and ordered her attention back to the man called Barney. He had a walkie-talkie, too.

"Take this chair, Miranda." He seated her beside Patricia and finished explaining what she had to do.

It seemed easy enough, and she told him so.

He grinned. "Very easy, until all four regular lines are ringing at once and the network people start arriving with a hundred questions and two hundred problems. If we're tied up, you use this phone. When the White House operator answers, ask her to connect you with...."

Miranda looked across the room at the phone he indicated. Under the plastic strip below the buttons, where the number would normally be, was a small silhouette of one of the most famous houses in the world. The words "White House" were printed beside the tiny picture.

She looked up in astonishment to meet the amused expression in the man's eyes. "You mean this is—"

"A direct line," he assured her. "When things get hectic around here, you may have to use it. You'll be familiar with the routine by then. But for now, just take down the information and give it to one of the men in 101." For the first time Miranda noticed a connecting door and heard voices from the room beyond.

At that moment Jake hung up and turned to her. "Miranda," he said in a low voice.

She met his eyes reluctantly, but when she

did she could see that his night had been troubled, too. "Yes, Jake?"

His brown eyes were tired, but intense with concern as they bore into hers. "Are you—"

Patricia interrupted before he could finish. "Jake, this lady would like to know if you could just leave her credentials at the desk of the motel." Her whisper was probably loud enough to be heard through her hand, which covered the receiver.

Jake reluctantly shifted his gaze from Miranda. He smiled and shook his head. "Sorry, Patricia. I can't even leave them with you. They must be picked up, in person, from an agent."

"Oh." The brunette head tilted to one side. "Then her brother-in-law couldn't collect them along with his, either, could he?"

"No way," Jake answered. Then he lowered his voice. "Is she giving you trouble?"

Patricia's curls swung horizontally. "No." She put the phone back to her ear. When she spoke again her tone was firm and decisive. "Credentials can only be distributed by a certified agent, Mrs. Austin. I'm sure you understand that we can take no chances." She listened for a minute before giving a decisive nod. "We'll see you then." She hung up. "Mrs. Austin decided she could make it on time, after all."

"Most of them do," Jake declared ironically. "Certified?" He grinned at her.

"It makes you sound more important," Patricia told him, looking puzzled when his laughter burst out. Both Miranda and Barney were seized with fits of coughing at the same time.

"I'll leave you to it," said Barney finally. "If you have any questions ask me or Patricia." He returned to his computer terminal.

Jake left through the open door behind him, but seconds later Miranda heard his voice from the next room. She fought down a tide of disappointment. He had been about to say something, maybe offer an apology.

She turned determinedly, smiling at her friend. "Are you an authority in such a short time?"

"I learned fast," Patricia dimpled. "This is fun."

"I'm glad you feel that way. I was afraid when I walked in here that I might have to apologize for volunteering you."

"It's a break from washing diapers." She lowered her voice to a conspirator's whisper. "Now tell me about Jake Stewart, Miranda."

Fortunately for Miranda three phones began to ring at once.

As the day wore on, the pace increased. It seemed that every weekly paper, every radio and cable TV station in South Georgia and North Florida had decided it wanted to send a representative to cover the president's visit. She wondered aloud about clearance for the media in the larger cities. Barney explained that they had received the information through the wire services and had already been approved through regular channels.

Jake didn't linger in the room next door. Miranda could have told almost to the minute when he'd gone, not only because of the absence of the bass-baritone, but by the loss of electricity in the air.

At noon one of the men, she thought his name was Merv, went for hamburgers. The phones never stopped ringing, and Miranda and Patricia took turns eating. Finally at five-thirty things began to slow down. "That's it for today, ladies," said Barney. "Be back in the morning at eight."

Miranda managed to come up with a plausible excuse for refusing Patricia's invitation to dinner. She knew that her friend couldn't wait to get her alone to pick at her about Jake, and she couldn't depend on her own ability to discuss her relationship—or lack of one—rationally. "We'll get together soon," she promised, waving Patricia away in her car.

When Miranda pulled into the driveway fifteen minutes later she turned off the ignition and sat for a moment in the car, dreading to go inside. The work had been good for her, had helped to take her mind off Jake, but here, with him so close, the memories of last night developed vividly in her mind.

Finally she got out. Did a curtain move in the window of the coach house? Deliberately she squared her shoulders and went inside. She headed directly for her bedroom and a bathing suit.

Ten laps of the pool helped. Ten more, and she felt almost human. She could put Jake Stewart out of her thoughts, out of her life with barely an effort, she told herself. Ten more laps and she began to think about food. That was always a good sign.

She swam to the shallow end of the pool and dipped her head under the water one last time to wash her streaming hair away from her face. Involuntarily her eyes went to the window again. There! The curtain had definitely moved. He was watching her. The realization gave her a certain sense of triumph. It wasn't going to be easy for him to put her out of his mind, either.

And why should he? She didn't care about social standing and money, so it shouldn't matter to him, either. Their feelings for each other were something very special indeed, and they shouldn't be so carelessly discarded. She wasn't quite ready to put a label on those feelings, but she knew she could easily fall in love with Jake. And from his response she thought he was in a similar state. Surely they should explore their emotions further. At least while he was here.

Could she make him change his mind? A slow curve softened the line of her mouth. Miranda had never set out deliberately to seduce a man before, but the idea had some merit. After all, he had done the same thing to her. What right did he have to call it off—she snapped her fingers—just like that? Who did he think he was? Maybe she could convince him that he was wrong about her.

Moving with studied grace in case he was still watching, she came up the steps of the pool, the water pouring off her body. She relaxed her hips slightly as she strolled to where her towel lay. Taking an inordinate amount of time, she dried every inch of herself. The thought of Jake watching her provoked another idea, a plan of action that she would have to think about for a while, but if it worked . . . .

The next morning found Miranda greeting the Secret Service team with a cheerful face. She had been quiet and reserved yesterday, in contrast to Patricia, but today she was openly charming.

She arrived with a picnic basket. "No greasy hamburgers today, gentlemen. Southern fried chicken and chocolate cake," she said swinging the basket under their noses before setting it out of the way.

They responded as she had known they would, with friendly smiles and warm grins. Home-cooked food seemed to loosen people up and she loved to cook. They were very nice men really.

The phones rang incessantly, but in between she learned more about each of them, and about Jake Stewart, who hadn't arrived yet. She didn't care that they realized she was attracted to Jake.

Barney was married. So was Emory, and his wife was expecting a baby. Merv was recently divorced and still showing the effects. She learned to her surprise that the turnover rate in the Secret Service was quite high. Merv himself provided that particular bit of information. He was ready to switch jobs, in hopes of getting his wife back. The Service was hard on a personal relationship, he had said dourly. He wanted to stay with the Treasury Department, maybe in the counterfeiting division, but more than anything he wanted to remarry his former wife.

Patricia overheard the conversation, and the suspicious gleam that had lit her blue eyes whenever Miranda mentioned Jake flared once again. "Miranda, I have to talk to you," she insisted. "In private."

They left the men to devour the contents of the picnic basket and answer the phones, and sat on the grassy lawn outside the motel room, eating their own share of the lunch.

"Miranda, I feel that I must warn you about Jake Stewart. I didn't want you to know we'd talked about you, but this is serious," Patricia said, holding her breath for the explosion.

To her utter amazement it didn't come. Patricia knew Miranda's aversion to gossip, particularly gossip about herself. She'd become hypersensitive during her divorce, and no wonder.

Now all she said was, "What did he say about me?"

Patricia's jaw dropped. "Well, er ... he said ...."

"I hope you didn't tell him any awful things, Patricia. Not any of the silly things we did growing up."

"Why, no. Of course not."

"Did you tell him that you thought I needed to have an affair?" Her teeth bit into the crispy chicken.

"Miranda!"

Miranda chewed for a moment. She laid the piece of chicken on one corner of her napkin and wiped her fingers delicately on another. "Why are you pretending to be shocked, Patricia? You've been telling me that for years." There was a militant gleam in her eye, but she was perfectly calm and in control.

"You're changing the subject, Miranda. I simply wanted to warn you against any permanent feelings for Jake. He is an attractive man, but you heard Merv. He said that the job is death on personal relationships."

Miranda looked at her friend. How could she possibly understand that the promise of hope, fragile as it was, wouldn't die that easily. Then she sighed. "He thinks we're too different, Patricia, that I've always been sheltered and protected."

"What?" her friend asked blankly.

"Well, that's part of it. Maybe money and background are another part, I don't know. Isn't it ironic? Charles married me to get his hands on my heritage. To Jake the whole scene is a handicap. Can you imagine? Me protected and sheltered? Mother and daddy would love that. They think I've always been too independent for my own good."

Patricia was hesitant in her next question. "Are you sure that's why?"

Miranda shrugged. "That's what he told me. Oh, Patricia. I'm very much afraid that I'm falling in love with him." Her voice was barely a whisper. It was quite a step for her to admit her feelings like this even to her friend—she had lived within her shell of self-sufficiency for so long. "Jake Stewart has definite opinions on marriage, and they are all negative."

Just then the subject of their conversation laughed from the room behind them. Miranda whipped her head around at the sound. But Jake was too far away to have heard her confession. She relaxed. She wasn't ready for him to know, not yet. She forced a smile. "Back to work," she said lightly and stood, brushing the grass from the back of her white slacks.

Jake stayed only long enough to check on their progress and to eat a piece of her cake. His compliment on her cooking was sincere, but his expression was even more guarded than usual.

The press began arriving the next morning. The president's plane, Air Force One, would touch down a the Naval Air Station in Jacksonville, Florida, at four-thirty. He would travel by helicopter from there to the small airport on St. Simons. By six o'clock, he should be settled at Donald's house.

Barney explained the timetable to Miranda and Patricia. "Members of the national media travel ahead of him in another plane, and except for the death watch, they'll be transported by bus."

"Death watch!?" both women exclaimed at the same time.

"That's what they call it," he answered with a

shake of his head. "The most senior correspondents are always on his plane or else their helicopter is in sight of his...in case anything happens."

"That's morbid," Miranda said heatedly.

Barney gave her a sad smile. "Why do you think our jobs exist, Miranda?"

A few of the network correspondents stopped by room 103 before they checked into their rooms. They had a thousand questions, it seemed to Miranda, things that any guide book could have explained. When she told a White House reporter from ABC that, he looked huffy.

His counterpart from NBC chuckled appreciatively and asked Patricia for a date.

She smiled sweetly and asked if she could bring her three children.

The man was taken aback for a minute but recovered quickly. He gave her a sheepish look. "If you like," he said with a grin. "Your husband, too."

Miranda and Patricia decided that they liked him.

"Why don't you bring the three children and husband over for a swim tonight when this is over," Miranda asked her friend later.

"Do you think Dan and the kids could get through your gate?" Miranda had explained the precautions Jake was taking around her parents' house.

Barney had been listening to their conversation. "I'll take care of it," he said kindly.

"Then we'd love to come."

"Good." Miranda had a sudden thought. "Barney, if you're off duty, why don't you come, too?"

"Thanks, anyway. My boss wouldn't like it, not the first night the president's here."

"Your boss?"

"Jake." He looked at her as though he would have liked to say more on the subject of Jake, but the telephones began to ring again.

Extra officials from all sorts of places were gathering for last-minute instructions—the highway patrol, county and city police, staff from the Atlanta headquarters of the Treasury Department, even from the Georgia Game and Fish Commission. All roads crossing the route that the president would take would be sealed off until he reached his destination.

Residents and guests on Sea Island are going to love this! Miranda thought wryly. The elegant resort wasn't accustomed to having its placidity disturbed, even by the president of the United States. She could imagine some of the comments, especially if the people commenting hadn't voted for him.

By the end of the afternoon everyone was beginning to look harried. Last-minute appeals for credentials had to be handled with tact and diplomacy, when Miranda would have loved to scold the tardy ones. She and Patricia tried to gather information quickly, so that the agents could clear as many of the dawdlers as possible. Finally at four-thirty they shut down their part of the operation and locked the door.

"Do you have a ride to the airport?" Miranda hadn't heard Jake come up behind her.

"Are we allowed to go?" she asked, turning to meet his gaze. He was wearing a dark-gray suit, white shirt and a navy tie with a subdued stripe. The tailoring was perfect. No one would suspect that a leather holster carried a wicked-looking revolver under the fine fabric, but she had caught a glimpse of him earlier, in his shirt-sleeves.

He reached into his coat pocket and pulled out a tiny bit of metal in a bright color, which he affixed to the collar of her blouse. She steeled herself against his touch.

"Of course you are," he said with more gentleness than she would have expected.

Tension wasn't exactly the word for the feelings she'd seen building slowly but relentlessly in the men throughout the afternoon. Expectancy? No. It was more than that. They were completely ready, that was it—prepared as thoroughly as it was humanly possible to be. Their eyes and ears and minds were honed to the finest sharpness, and some other sense—some sixth sense for want of a better term—was on ultimate alert.

Miranda's own sensibility picked it up immediately in Jake. How different it must be to live on the knife-edge of readiness like this. The pressure and stress must be overwhelming. No wonder, as Merv had told her, the turnover was high.

She realized that Jake's question was automatic, that she had been shunted to a different section of his mind, reserved for occasions such as this. But she didn't resent it. She knew that his intense focus was absolutely necessary, and she was strangely proud of him for being able to put all other thoughts and distractions entirely aside.

Men in overalls, some with children perched on their shoulders, rubbed elbows with housewives and professional types behind a rope barricade that lined the short drive into the airport. The local high-school band was there, resplendent in uniforms and sounding beautifully small-town America, as they played with all the enthusiasm of youth. The brilliant Georgia sun shone down on the colorful scene.

"Who got the band their clearance?" laughed Patricia.

"I don't know," Miranda answered, but the remark made her think. There must be a lot more to security than handing out press credentials.

The small metal badges they wore entitled the two women to join the mayor and other dignitaries who would greet the president. But Patricia spotted her husband in the crowd. "I see Dan," she said, waving to him eagerly. "We'll see you tonight, Miranda."

"Sure," Miranda answered, distracted as a sudden awareness silenced the throngs of people. *My gosh*, she thought, *how many times have I heard or read that hackneyed phrase "A hush fell over the crowd"? But it's totally apt.*

The unmistakable sound of rotors heralded the arrival of one of the most powerful leaders of the world, and the realization silenced the mass of people who, only moments before, had been laughing and talking. Even young children, who surely couldn't understand, were caught in the awesome spell.

Miranda blinked suddenly, inspired by a loyalty and love for her country that she didn't normally think about. But at a moment like this she could not help but be overwhelmed with appreciation for what this single man stood for.

A slight breeze stirred the flag that flew over the small airport terminal as the first helicopter appeared over the horizon. Another, smaller one followed, but not too closely. The lead aircraft resembled a huge ungainly insect, and it hovered precariously in the air before descending slowly to light with surprising grace on the tarmac.

Then the stairs were down, the band struck up "Hail to the Chief" and the people laughed and cheered, released as one by the appearance at the top of the steps of the president himself. His physical presence seemed to remind them that he was one of them, granted his place in history by their vote.

The president didn't hurry. He strolled leisurely along the line of waiting dignitaries and stopped to chat for a minute with each of them, as though he'd waited all day for the pleasure. Donald Webster walked just behind him, introducing him to people he hadn't met before.

When the two men reached Miranda, she had to take a restorative breath before she could respond to his friendly greeting. "How do you do, Mr. President?" She resisted the urge to curtsy and swallowed a giggle at the thought.

He might have read her mind. A glimmer of laughter appeared in his eyes. "You are as beautiful as your mother, Miranda."

It was the last thing she'd expected him to say and she blinked. "Sir?"

"I stayed for a few days with my friend here during the campaign. I met your parents then."

Donald leaned forward for the kiss with which he always greeted Miranda. He laughed. "I think your father was a little bit jealous. We'll see you at the house, my dear."

They moved on and Miranda was left to stare after them speculatively. If the handsome widower had flirted with her mother, she could see how her father might have been jealous. He would be a charismatic man even without the power of the presidency behind him.

Miranda was brought out of her reverie by the sight of a dark head above the crowd. Jake was speaking into his walkie-talkie. She saw his head swivel in an impatient shake. He took off in a run after the presidential party, and her heart bounded in her chest. But it was a loping run. Nothing in his expression indicated danger, just disgust.

Then she saw the reason for his irritation. Ever the politician, the president had waded into the crowd and was shaking hands with all sorts of people who had no security clearance. Of course he was surrounded by men in conservative suits with guns under their jackets, but he occasionally slithered from behind their protective backs, with a smile of pure enjoyment.

Miranda's mouth mirrored the smile. But she also felt a pang of sympathy for the Secret Service staff.

At last the president had climbed into a long black limousine, and was moving away from the airport amid the scream of sirens. The crowd began to clear.

Miranda made her way to her car, feeling very lonely for some reason that she refused to analyze. Decisively she opened the door and climbed in. She was having company tonight and there was a lot to do.

The children were delighted to be invited to "Aunt" Miranda's, and "Aunt" Miranda felt guilty for not having had them sooner. She had been there for a whole week. And except for the last two days, her thoughts and energy had been completely dominated by a man who now didn't want to bother with her.

Kaye and Kevin, already wearing their tiny flotation rings, scurried to the shallow end of the pool. Miranda took the baby, Kerby, and nuzzled his sweet, powder-scented neck. "Hi, Dan," she greeted Patricia's husband.

Dan was a dear, quiet man, the perfect foil for his wife's vivaciousness. "How are you, Miranda?" he asked.

"Fine," she answered, ignoring Patricia's snort.

She and Patricia left the two older children by the pool with Dan and went to the kitchen for cold drinks. They were both subdued, agreeing that they had heard enough talk in the last two days to last a lifetime. The quiet was a blessed one.

Miranda was content to hold the baby in her arms, letting Patricia get out ice and cola. But finally her irrepressible friend could no longer hold her tongue or her curiosity. "Have you talked to Jake?"

Miranda shrugged. "Not any more than you have," she said stiffly.

"Don't, Miranda." Patricia's voice sounded slightly choked.

Miranda turned to look at her and was astonished to find her eyes swimming with tears. "I can't stand to see you hurting," she went on. "You went through enough pain with Bastard Charles." She had always like to give Charles a title.

Miranda gave her a warm, grateful hug with her free arm. "You're the best friend a woman could have." She had to blink a bit herself. "But don't worry about me. I'll be okay."

"I've seen you watch him and you know what? — you *are* in love with him."

Miranda drew back, horrified. "Does it show that clearly?"

"Not to someone who doesn't know you," Patricia hastily reassured her.

"He is the most maddening man," Miranda commented, trying for lightness. "I really don't know what I'm going to do about him."

The toddlers still played in the shallow end of the pool, but Dan was no longer alone. "Uh-oh. Speak of the devil," murmured Patricia as she stepped through the door.

Miranda was thankful for the warning. It gave her time to compose her features.

Dan and Jake had evidently introduced themselves. They were talking like old friends, but broke off the conversation to stand when the two women approached.

Jake felt like he had just been punched in the stomach. He was breathless at the sight of Miranda with a child in her arms. She was so damned beautiful that he couldn't tear his eyes away. The baby's chubby fingers reached for a fiery strand of hair and pulled sharply. She laughed and disentangled his grip. Her lips pressed a gentle kiss to his cheek as Dan reached for his son. Jake watched the tableau, unable to rationalize his envy.

"Hello, Jake," she said calmly when Kerby was safely ensconced in his father's arms.

"Hello, Miranda," he answered. For the first time in their acquaintance he seemed ill at ease.

"Can I get you a cold drink?" she asked politely.

Patricia held the tray toward her husband, who balanced the baby in one arm and took a glass. But her bright eyes switched from Jake to

Miranda. Kaye and Kevin came running up just then to reach for their own drinks.

"No. I can't stay."

Then why did you come? Miranda wanted to scream. They certainly couldn't talk now. *Why didn't you wait until I was alone? Don't you know how much I want your arms around me?*

Don't you know how much I want to hold you? thought Jake. Why had he come? He must have been insane! Except that being around her for the last few days and not being able to touch her, to talk to her in any but the most casual way, had been harder than anything he'd ever been through.

Tonight, when the president had said he would spend the evening dining alone with his friend, Jake had been drawn through the gate in the hedge by a powerful need, one that was now frustrated by the presence of her friends. He felt like an intruder. And yet he'd seen the same hunger in her eyes . . . for a minute.

This was a gigantic mistake. If he didn't get out of here he was going to pull some ridiculous caveman trick, like throwing her over his shoulder and disappearing into the bushes with her. "I just came over to thank the two of you for all your help these past few days," he said hurriedly.

"We enjoyed the experience." Patricia spoke for both of them, but her tone was none too amicable.

"Good night then," Jake said in a low voice. He turned to go, but there was a strong, strange magnetism that seemed to emanate from Miranda. He looked over his shoulder, and their eyes locked for a timeless moment.

"Good night, Jake," she whispered finally, releasing both of them.

When he had disappeared through the gate, Dan looked bewilderedly at his wife. "I'm not sure a hacksaw would have cut the tension. Can someone explain?"

"Don't ask," ordered Patricia.

8

"I WOULD LIKE TO SEE A BIKINI — one of your more daring ones," Miranda told the saleswoman determinedly. It was the only kind of bathing suit that would work for her scheme.

However, when she saw the incredibly flimsy material in the woman's hand she almost changed her mind. Surely that wasn't a bathing suit! She sent her a look of mute horror, but the saleswoman simply nodded. "This is one of our latest models."

When Miranda had donned the tiny scraps of flesh-colored cloth, she scrutinized herself carefully in the mirror. Impressive, she had to admit. But her inhibitions were still operational. "Do you have a beach robe?" she asked through the curtain of the dressing room.

"Yes," the woman answered. "We have one that just came in — it's black."

The robe was of a lacy fabric, just sheer enough to hint at the curves underneath. It covered her body from mid-thigh to just below her throat. The flowing sleeves were graceful and feminine.

"I'll take it," Miranda said, making the decision before she could change her mind.

"It looks terrific!" the woman enthused.

"Does it?" As long as it didn't look really ridiculous she was satisfied.

Fifteen minutes later she left the small specialty shop with packages in hand and walked the three blocks back to the house.

As she approached the gates the man standing beside them straightened and then relaxed. Two other men sat in a car with the door open. One of them put a microphone to his lips and began to speak in inaudible tones. Reporting her whereabouts, she supposed. After three days of presidential presence she should be accustomed to having her movements charted.

The Secret Service knew exactly where anyone who might have the slightest connection with the president was at any given moment. She planned to lever a bit of that knowledge out of them right now. Her courage had been strengthened by the discovery of Jake's real feelings the night the Sanders family had come for a swim. He could deny it until doomsday but Jake Stewart was almost as much in love with her as she was with him. She was convinced of it. Now if she could only convince him that falling in love wasn't the first step to perdition.

"Good morning, Miss Woodbarry," the man at the gate greeted her.

"Good morning, Steve. I wonder, do you know Jake's schedule today," she asked idly.

"He's on duty now. He should be finished for the day around two."

"Thanks." She continued down the drive, swinging her packages. So far, so good, she thought. Except for the time. Her tan wasn't developed enough for her to stay in the hot midday sun for long. Hopefully Jake would respond immediately. But if he didn't she was resigned to endure the pain of too many ultraviolet rays. Because she knew this was her last chance, and she intended it to be successful, even if it took all afternoon.

THE SUN BLASTED DOWN like a furnace as Miranda approached the pool with the robe over her arm, a glass of lemonade in one hand and a book and sunglasses in the other. She had decided against using sunscreen. It wasn't at all becoming to present yourself greased and shining like a pig ready for roasting when your intention was seduction.

She had come to the conclusion that Jake Stewart was worth whatever she had to undertake. She did not intend to let this man walk out of her life easily, even at the risk of making a fool of herself.

She was going to fight for him. If her weapons were unorthodox... well, they had been used for centuries by women a lot craftier than she. She had been extensively trained in the art of theater, and now she planned to put some of that training to use. The one response she could be sure of was a physical one, so that would be her starting point.

Jake was everything desirable in a man—intelligent, honest, strong and tender at the same time—and she loved him quite desperately. She'd never felt this way before. Her feelings for Charles were easily recognizable in retrospect as infatuation. She had followed him around like the dazed teenager she was, caught up in a dream of romance.

Jake was reality. The woman she'd become was wide awake now and determined to show him that they belonged together. But first she had to get his attention.

She sighed heavily and dropped the robe on a chair. The tall glass of lemonade almost slid from her nervous fingers, but she managed to set it on an umbrella table beside the pool, along with the paperback book.

Her long copper tresses had been wound on top of her head and secured with a comb. She'd freed teasing tendrils at her nape to soften the style, but wet stringy hair was not part of the seductive image she was striving for.

The bikini helped. It was modest in cut, as bikinis go, but on her figure the scraps of cloth seemed to shrink to almost nothing. However, she had done all her pulling and tugging inside the house. Now she meant to wear the thing as though she were perfectly comfortable in it.

She strolled leisurely toward the shallow end of the pool. That was where she'd stood the day she saw the curtain move. She dipped one toe into the water and glanced up through the screen of her lashes. Nothing...the curtain didn't stir. He should be in his room by now, off duty and receptive.

Slowly she slid into the water up to her neck, careful to keep her hair dry. The water was blessedly cool compared to the outside air, but she couldn't stay too long. Smelling like chlorine was not part of her plan either.

The depth here was less than three feet, so she sat on the bottom, her hands on either side of her hips. She let her legs float almost to the surface and risked another glance. There! She was sure she'd seen something.

Playfully she skimmed the water with one hand, trying with all the élan she could muster to look completely casual and unaware of any watching eyes. Give it another five minutes. Her nose was beginning to feel the effects of the sun in just this short length of time. Soon she would be forced to put on the robe, but not yet.

Moving slowly, she stood. The water sloshed around her thighs. She climbed the steps to the concrete verge and strolled back around to the umbrella table. She was hoping that Jake wouldn't be able to resist the blatant invitation she was about to deliver to join her by the pool.

Jake was drawn to the window as he always was when he got off duty. The off-chance that he might catch a glimpse of Miranda pulled at him like a magnet, and he was unable to resist the temptation.

Suddenly he pushed the curtain aside, abusing the fabric in his clenched fist. Dammit! She was naked! What the hell was she doing? As he watched, she stretched out on a chaise lounge, and he realized that her body was barely covered by the most indecent bathing suit he'd ever laid eyes on.

She was practically naked! As he watched she took the comb from her hair. The whole blasted glory came tumbling down around her shoulders. His fingers itched to bury themselves in the mass of flame. He could close his eyes and remember the scent of wild flowers.

Jake plunged his hands into his pockets. His eyes were glued to her. He couldn't look away. That suit would leave very little to anyone's imagination, and his was vividly activated by his memories of her body. His desire grew to unbearable intensity as he watched her.

She perched her sunglasses on her nose and picked up a book. The lounge was partially shaded by the wide striped umbrella, but her shapely calves were unprotected. Lazily, she lifted one knee and the move sent a white-hot dagger of physical need through him. He groaned aloud.

"Did you say something, Jake?" a masculine voice asked from the next room.

He could hear the hoarseness in his own voice when he replied. "No, Barney."

Barney came to the door. "Something up?"

Jake heard the footstep of his friend on the hard floor. Barney couldn't see Miranda like that! He dropped the curtain and turned. "It's nothing!" he said sharply.

But the Secret Service agent in Barney was not to be deterred. He joined Jake at the window, and pushed aside the curtain. "It's Miranda," he said fondly.

As Jake watched, Barney automatically checked out the surrounding landscape before returning his gaze to Miranda's reclining figure. "Poor kid. Imagine having this paradise at your front door and being so fair you have to cover yourself up."

Jake's head jerked around to look again. She had put on some kind of robe and was tying a sash at her waist. It was a thin thing, but at least it was better than the bikini. He gave a sigh of relief and relaxed, but the additional covering wasn't effective against the mental pictures that his mind was conjuring up. "Only until July," he answered absently, suddenly and painfully remembering the way her breast curved in his palm.

"July?"

"She's careful about getting too much sun." He knew that his words weren't making sense, but his mind pictures had moved to the soft feminine dip of her waist.

"Then what's she doing out now?" asked Barney.

Jake gave a shrug in an effort to dispel the image of her smooth skin, her flat stomach. "I don't know."

"I like her. She's quite a woman."

"Yeah." All woman. She smells like heaven, tastes like a slice of honey dipped peach. . . .

"And has more than a casual interest in you."

The words finally brought Jake back to his senses. He massaged the stiffness in the back of his neck. "Dammit! Barney, you know how I feel about marriage."

Barney's brows rose. "Marriage?" he questioned mildly as he crossed his arms over his chest. "Were we talking about marriage? I thought you preferred informal relationships."

"I do! That's the problem. Miranda is marriage bait if I ever saw it." Jake couldn't control the magnetic pull of the woman outside. His eyes went to the window again. His voice dropped an octave. "Barney, you know how I feel. This is no life for a woman."

"Some of them manage," Barney said dryly.

"Your marriage is an exception. But can you honestly say that Eva wouldn't rather you be at home every night?"

"Eva loves me, and I love her. We can't have everything, but we take what we can and we're happier married than apart. It's better than nothing."

Jake waited for him to elaborate, but Barey simply shrugged. "I wonder if that sun is as hot as it looks?" he said enigmatically, and left the room.

Jake pushed the curtain aside. The little fool. She was going to have second-degree burns if she didn't . . . oh, hell!

What he saw below provoked a sharp epithet.

The heat was sapping Miranda's energy. She'd been outside for almost an hour. What had seemed like a good idea in the cool morning hours now could be perceived as the greatest folly. She wiped the perspiration from her upper lip and sat up, preparing to return to the comfort of air conditioning.

Her back was to the house next door but, when she heard the creak of the gate, her heart gave a tremendous leap. At last! She swiveled her head, and only shock froze the wide welcoming smile on her face.

The man who approached was certainly not Jake. *Dear God, what have I done to deserve this,* she cried to herself.

Here I sit, in the middle of this farce, *this theater of the absurd, about to welcome the president of the United States of America with almost no clothes on!* She checked to be sure that the robe was tied securely. "Good morning," she greeted him, calmly but erroneously since it was afternoon.

He grinned, her nervousness not escaping him. "How are you, Miranda?" He was dressed in khaki shorts and a navy knit shirt. It was difficult not to notice his strong physique. He was in his mid-sixties but had obviously kept in shape.

"I'm fine, sir. And you? W-won't you sit down?"

He nodded, folding his very fit body into the chair beside the chaise. Miranda gulped. Suddenly she remembered that the president had two daughters. One of them was a bit of a rebel, too. He had probably seen a bikini before.

"Can . . . may . . . would you like a glass of lemonade?"

"Thank you, yes, if I wouldn't be interrupting."

She looked at him blankly, and he indicated the book in her hand.

Miranda had completely forgotten the book. In fact she couldn't have even quoted the title. She dropped it on the grass. "It isn't a very good story. I'm afraid the author's premise is lost on me."

"I agree. Especially the idea of swapping the president for a look-alike."

"You've read it?" Miranda relaxed a fraction. He seemed more interested in the bestseller than in her discomfort.

"I have and I can assure you that the Secret Service wouldn't stand for a swap."

She returned his warm smile and stood keeping the edges of the robe in an iron fist. "That's reassuring and easily believable, having witnessed their thoroughness firsthand. Excuse me. I'll get your lemonade."

When she returned moments later her smile was natural and she was much more comfortable. "Here you are," she said handing him the glass.

He took a long swallow and sighed. "Thank you. It's delicious. One of the men, Barney I believe, says your chocolate cake is superb, too." For just a minute he sounded like a wistful boy.

Miranda leaned back against the cushion and chuckled. She slid the sunglasses off her nose and perched them on top of her head. "Would that be a hint, Mr. President?"

"As broad a one as you've ever heard," he laughed. "But as a matter of fact I've come as deputy for my host to ask you to join two old bachelors for dinner this evening."

"And I'm to furnish dessert?"

"If you should be so inclined," he answered with a twinkle in his eye that belied the dignity of his reply. He took another long swallow and set the glass down on the table between them.

"I would be charmed to have dinner with you," she said with equal formality. "And bring dessert."

"Donald also suggested you bring a date if you like, but I'm afraid he forgot all the disadvantages of having me for a guest." He sighed and slid down more comfortably in the chair. His fingers made a tower under his chin and his eyes took on a faraway look.

She had seen the pose in interviews conducted in the Oval Office. He might be behind his desk right now, contemplating a matter of worldwide importance, rather than trying to explain why it would be difficult for her to bring a date. "It's all right, Mr. President. I understand. I'm not dating anyone who would be disappointed at not being included," she told him gently.

The clear gaze swung to her. "That's right. You helped the Secret Service clear the local press, didn't you?"

"Yes, sir. It was quite an education." She

smiled and her gaze dropped to her fingers, tangled in her lap. *One I'll never forget and possibly never recover from,* she added to herself.

He seemed to sense the sadness in her, but didn't pursue the subject. "Then I won't feel guilty at monopolizing your evening. Donald said to come at seven. I'll look forward to hearing about your parents' trip. Where are they? In Europe?"

"Yes. Daddy was invited to speak at a seminar, and mother talked him into making it a long vacation." And she missed them. For the first time she realized how much.

"Your father is a lucky man." He looked out over the dunes to the horizon, with that same contemplative expression in his eyes. "I lost my wife five years ago, while I was still in the Senate."

"I remember reading about her. She must have been a remarkable woman."

"She was," he agreed softly and chuckled. "She would have loved living in the White House, but she'd have given the Secret Service fits."

Suddenly the president slapped the arms of his chair lightly and stood, breaking the somber mood. "Thanks for the lemonade, Miranda, and the conversation." He shaded his eyes and lifted his face toward the sun. "Aren't you afraid you'll get burned?" he asked.

The comment reminded her of the purpose of this farce. She had already been burned, very badly. She stood, too. "Yes, sir. I'm going inside now." The dejected tone of her voice earned her a sharp glance, which she met with a smile. "I'll be looking forward to this evening."

But he was too astute to be put off with a social platitute. "Something is bothering you." When she didn't answer he went on as though she had. "Troubles with a young man?"

She chuckled. "He isn't exactly young. He's in his thirties . . . I guess." It dawned on her suddenly that she had no idea how old Jake was. "I'm not exactly sure."

The president chuckled, too. "If he's in his thirties, he's young." He put one hand casually in the pocket of his shorts, and his voice took on a note of seriousness. "But you don't know how much time you will be given together, Miranda. You shouldn't keep him dangling. Being by yourself is no way to live."

She bit deeply into her lower lip to keep from laughing hysterically at his misconception. If only Jake were hers to dangle. "Yes, sir," she finally managed.

"I'll see you this evening."

She watched him leave, sympathizing at the loneliness in him. The tremendous burden of the office he held kept him surrounded with people. He was never alone, but still he was lonely because the one person he needed wasn't there.

As soon as he disappeared through the gate, she began gathering up her things. She remembered the president's words: "Being by yourself is no way to live." Her sun-kissed skin was a stinging reminder that she had tried. At least she wouldn't look back in regret because she'd done nothing.

For now she'd better get inside and bathe her face in vinegar. Balancing a glass in each hand and the book under her arm, she crossed the lawn to the side door, which led into the study.

"Well, that was some show!" a harsh voice declared from behind her.

She whirled, one glass slipping from her fingers to spill its ice cubes and bounce harmlessly on the grass. "Jake!" she exclaimed, her lips parting in a smile. "You startled me. What did you say?"

"I said that was quite a performance." He bent to retrieve the glass.

When he straightened, her smile faded at the sight of his furious expression. What right did he have to be angry?

He reached in front of her to open the door. "After you," he said curtly.

Her first inclination was to slam the door in his face, but she restrained herself. This was the result she had hoped to gain from her ridiculous exercise of the afternoon. If he felt anger rather than desire, at least he was reacting with some kind of emotion. The few times she'd seen him since the president's arrival he'd been stone.

"Thank you," she said coolly. She didn't even glance back as she preceded him through the room to the hall and toward the kitchen.

"Would you like to explain what the hell that little act was all about?" He slammed the glass down on the table.

She dumped everything, too, and turned to brush by him. She didn't intend to play another scene in that kitchen. "I don't know what you're talking about," she said, reverting to another age-old womanly wile, which was nonetheless convenient.

He moved out of her way and followed her back down the hall into the living room. "Will you stop moving around, dammit?"

She remembered reading somewhere that you had the advantage if your back was to the light. With regal precision she crossed to the windows and turned to face him.

"Get that patrician nose out of the air," he ordered harshly. "You know damn well what I mean. Entertaining the president, in that scrap of nothing I presume you call a bathing suit!" He planted his fists on his hips. "You're practically naked, and he's old enough to be your father, Miranda."

"You think I..." she sputtered. "I am not naked!" she shouted belligerantly, holding her arms in their wide sleeves out from her sides.

"I saw that show you were putting on outside. Hollywood missed a great actress. That was a deliberate attempt at seduction if I've ever seen one."

"But not for him!" she cried defensively, and then shut her mouth in horror at the admission. She could barely meet his eyes, and when she did, their penetrating gaze sank her spirits more deeply.

A thick silence descended. "So it was me you were trying to seduce." His voice was dangerously low.

"Well, yes. But you seduced me first," she reminded him, striving to maintain her composure.

"As I remember it," he growled brusquely, "you were a willing victim, even to the point of doing a little 'advance preparation.'"

Memories of that night weakened her, brought forth reminiscences that heated her blood, kindled her desire, and prompted her heart to recall his loving side. Unable to come up with an answer, she finally had to turn away, embarrassed at his infiltrating gaze.

This wasn't the way she'd imagined this scene. She'd hoped they would be in each other's arms, not at each other's throats. She didn't want to fight with him, not now, when time was so short. "Only because I didn't want to have little cankerworms and polywogs," she said in a quiet voice.

There was silence behind her—then a husky chuckle. "That was *some* curse," he admitted.

She risked a glance and a weak smile over her shoulder. "I had barely started. If those men hadn't appeared with guns...." She shook her head. "I've never been so shocked in my life."

His fists, which had been planted on his hips in a hostile attitude, slowly unfolded. His fingers spread and slid into his pockets. "Shocked? Not frightened?" he asked.

She turned fully to look at him and was surprised to see the speculation in his half smile. Her own was puzzled. "Well, yes. A little frightened, too. But more than that, I was amazed. I had never seen a gun on Sea Island before."

He didn't seem to have a reply. Shifting a little, a small uneasy movement, he let his eyes drop to contemplate his well-shined shoes. When he raised his gaze to hers again, she felt hope bloom in her chest. His expression was tender. "Miranda."

The word was delivered in a voice soft and hungry, slightly bothered but full of longing; and it was all she needed to send her into his arms. She was enfolded closely, gently, in an embrace that was so caring, so comfortable, it brought tears to her eyes.

"Honey." He spoke over her head. When she would have drawn back to look up at him, he forestalled the movement by cradling her head under his chin. "No. Let me talk." He took a long breath. "This effect you have on me . . . I don't like it, Miranda. I'm very fond of you, but I told you before that we're too different."

His hand slid down her spine in a restless caress. On the return journey it paused at the center of her back. He tilted his head to look down at her accusingly. He lifted the hem of the beach robe. "When did you change bathing suits?" he demanded.

"When I came inside to fix the president a glass of lemonade," she answered with pretended innocence.

"I wish I'd known. It would have saved me some disturbing moments," he said wryly. Then his face twisted with emotion. "I want you. Miranda, I want you desperately!" His arms came around her, binding her in a constrictive circle, and his voice was a hoarse whisper in her hair. "You don't have to seduce me. Every time I see you . . . . But you must know that there can never be more than this."

Finally he cupped her face in his large hand, lifting it to look into her eyes. "Do you understand?"

"No," she said softly. "I don't understand. Some of your co-workers are married."

"But most of them have had problems. I had a friend like a second father, whose wife made his life hell. They loved each other, but it was hard for them to live with her fear. Harry got in the way of an assassination attempt. When she learned of his death, she took her own life."

"But, Jake . . . ."

"There's no point in discussing it, Miranda."

He was visibly withdrawing from her, and she didn't know how to stop him. "I'm not afraid, Jake. I'll take what you want to give me," she told him seriously.

His eyes narrowed in confusion. "What are you talking about?"

"I mean that I love you. If we have only a night, or a week, or . . . whatever we have together, I'll take it." Her lips tilted in a rueful smile. "It's better than nothing." She could hardly believe the words she'd spoken and opened her mouth to take them back. But something in Jake's eyes stopped her.

"Do you really mean that?" he whispered, obviously shaken.

Did she? Was she really ready to settle for a bit of passion as a substitute for commitment? Or was she living proof of hope springing eternal? Hope that he would change his mind, that she could show him, with the depth of her feelings, how precious and rare a love such as this really was? "Yes, I do," she breathed.

"What kind of woman are you?" The question wasn't the insult that the words might have suggested, for his voice was hushed with wonder.

Miranda looked into the deep, dark eyes serenely. "I'm a woman like all others, sometimes weak, often strong—"

"No!" he interrupted, pulling her to him with rough affection. "Not like any other woman."

She freed her arms from between their bodies to wind them around his neck. He lifted her off her feet until their eyes were level. He searched for something in the depths of her tranquil gaze. Finally his heavy lashes fell, and his mouth sought her parted lips with a gasp of hunger.

Her response was immediate and eager. She had opened the gate to her heart, and now she opened the gate to her emotions and her passion as well. Her hands combed through his thick hair, reveling in the tactile sensation.

Slowly he let her slide down the length of his body until her toes touched the floor while their lips clung. At last he released her lips to catch his breath against the soft skin of her cheek. His hand stroked her hair and she could feel it tremble. "I want to make love to you now."

"I want that, too, Jake."

He stepped back and took great pains to untie the sash at her waist without knotting it; his hands were shaking so. He slid it off her shoulders.

She helped with the suit, and when she finally stood before him, her long limbs glowing in the sunlight streaming from the window, he sighed. "You are so beautiful. This time I'm afraid we won't make it to the bedroom." he whispered and lifted her in his arms. "Do you mind?"

"Not a bit," she answered shakily.

Jake's eyes never broke contact with hers as he crossed the room to lay her gently on the plump cushions of the sofa. He stood back to jerk impatiently at his tie, his blood heating as he raked her form. His breathing accelerated sharply when his eyes stopped to linger on the curved mounds of her breasts. Her legs shifted, drawing his attention to the shadow at the apex of her thighs, and his breath halted completely. His jacket hit the floor.

Feeling clumsy he shed the rest of his clothes. Miranda seemed only slightly disconcerted at the sight of the revolver in its leather holster, but he was suddenly self-conscious of the weapon.

He put it under a table out of the line of her vision and quickly finished undressing. When he came down beside her she welcomed him with a confident smile and arms spread wide.

He caught his breath at the love shining out through her jade-green eyes and faltered for a moment. "Miranda. Honey, are you sure?" he murmured.

Instead of answering she slid one of those long smooth thighs between his legs and he was lost to all rational thought.

He moaned from deep within his throat. He wanted to hold her closely, so closely, to absorb her heat, her scent, her sweetness. His hands began to move restlessly over her, undirected, with a life of their own, to touch and stroke every inch of her satin skin. His lips followed to kiss softly the warm pulse in her throat, to take gentle mock bites of the delicately tinted crests of her breasts, to taste with a flick of his tongue the velvet skin of her belly.

He felt her ignite under his hands, his mouth. For a moment that seemed to stretch into eternity his fingers lingered at the warm moist center of her desire. She whimpered into the side of his neck as he drew patterns there.

"Jake!" Miranda heard the demand in the little whisper which burst from her lips. She began to move wildly, passionately, her nails digging into the muscular shoulders, impatient to stir the same ardent feelings in him.

"Honey!" he gasped. "Wait, sweetheart. I'll hurt you."

But she was beyond waiting; her hunger had burst all bounds. Her body arched upward into his hands.

Their joining was exciting and intense, and their bodies moved impulsively in mounting erotic rhythm, until the magnitude of his final thrust sent them both over the edge of reality into a heavenlike fantasy world. She clung to him, intoxicated, calling his name.

When she finally opened her eyes, he was leaning over her, smoothing the tangled mass of her hair away from her face, whispering sweet encouragement. . . .

He rolled to his side to relieve her of his weight. She shivered, fighting a vague sense of loss though he still held her close.

"Are you cold, honey?"

She heard the deep voice through her cheek where it rested against his chest. She shook her head. "No." But she was. She was cold and lonely on the inside with the fear of losing him.

Jake pulled the Afghan over them and they dozed for a short time. When they awoke they dressed, their movements reluctant and slow Jake pulled her into his arms and rested his cheek against hers.

She pulled away with a little cry. "Ouch."

His lips were suspiciously straight but he didn't make the obvious comment. She touched her cheek lightly. "I don't think I'm too badly burned. I'll bathe my face in vinegar. That always takes the sting out."

"And makes a great perfume," he added with a grin.

"I know," she said sadly. "I'll smell awful."

He started to cradle her face in his hands but thought better of it. Instead he slid his fingers into her hair and tilted her head up for a feather-light kiss. "That's okay. I like tossed salad. While you're taking care of your face I'll go next door and change clothes. We can have an early dinner at The Plantation and come back here for dessert."

Miranda winced. "I can't," she said in a small voice.

"Why not?" he asked. A possessive glimmer marred his gaze as he raised his head.

She liked that. "The president beat you to it. And I have to bake him a chocolate cake."

His arms tightened around her and he began to laugh helplessly. "Do you mean that you went to all that trouble to seduce me and then accepted a dinner date with someone else?"

"It isn't easy to say no to the president, Jake. Besides I didn't think you were coming."

"I hope he likes tossed salad," he teased but his smile was slightly off center as he released her. "It's probably for the best. We'll have time to think about what we're going to do."

"Do?" she asked.

"Yeah." He didn't sound enthusiastic as he added, "'Advance preparation,' remember? When we can see each other, where."

She didn't want him to have time to think. If past experience was anything to go on, he would only think of reasons why they shouldn't be together. "When are you leaving? Tomorrow?" she asked.

He shook his head and backed away from her, shoving his hands into his pockets. "No. The president leaves tomorrow. I'm leaving the next morning for Detroit."

"Oh, yes. I remember your telling me. Your vacation with your stepfather." She wanted to beg him to stay, but she wouldn't.

"Would you like to have dinner tomorrow night after he's on the plane?" Jake asked almost hesitantly.

Her green eyes glistened with unbidden tears. "Okay," she said. Then she had a thought. "He said I could bring a date tonight if he were cleared for security," she added hopefully.

"No, honey. I'll wait my turn."

9

THE TELEPHONE ROUSED MIRANDA from a sound sleep. She turned over to find herself tangled hopelessly in the sheet. "Drat!" she muttered groggily and finally managed to extricate one arm. By that time she was thoroughly irritated. "Hello!" she barked into the phone.

A husky chuckle greeted her. "Good morning, sunshine."

She snuggled the receiver to her ear and buried the other half of her face in the pillow. "It isn't morning," she informed Jake in a muffled voice, still hoarse with sleep. "It's still dark."

"Your shades are down. It's almost eight."

She raised her head and opened one eyelid a crack. Sure enough, there was a thin line of bright sunlight under the edge of the lowered shade.

"Honey, I'm calling to tell you that I probably won't see you until tonight," he went on. "The helicopter leaves at five to take the president to Jacksonville. My vacation starts as soon as he's off the ground but it will take me an hour or so to attend to a few things and get back here. Okay?"

Miranda had flipped onto her back during the course of his monologue. Now she was smiling. This was the first time Jake had bothered to inform her about his plans, and the implications warmed her. "Okay," she said very softly, very seductively, into the phone.

"Miranda. Have you gone back to sleep?" he demanded loudly.

Men! So much for seduction in her husky tones. She smiled and shook her head. "No, Jake. I heard you. I'll see you tonight."

She expected him to hang up, his mission having been completed, but he surprised her again. "How was your evening?"

The evening had been fine but the night long. Getting to sleep had seemed an impossibility. A strange ache to have Jake beside her had grown to a full-fledged pain when she realized how short their time together was growing. When sleep had finally claimed her it was fractured with dark dreams. Soon he would be gone, leaving her without a backward glance. Once again she felt the coldness invade her limbs, the same coldness that had caused her to shiver in his arms yesterday. "The president is a very nice man, and Donald is always charming," she told him, her voice toneless and formal.

There was silence on the other end of the line. "Miranda, have you changed your mind?" he finally asked quietly. "I can take a plane out tonight."

She squeezed her lids tightly shut and clutched the phone. This was her chance. She should say yes. She should tell him to go. "No, I haven't changed my mind," she said. *God help me.* "I'll see you about six?"

"Around that time. Don't worry if I'm late."

"All right."

"Bye, honey." He hung up.

How domestic the words sounded. "Don't worry if I'm late." She replaced the receiver and sat up wearily, hugging her bent legs, resting her cheek on her knees. What kind of heartache was she letting herself in for?

THE AROMA OF ROASTING BEEF filled the air. Miranda squeezed the bulb of the baster, drawing the juices up from the bottom of the pan into the plastic tube. She saturated the rib roast as well as the potatoes and carrots arranged around it and closed the oven door.

Her face was flushed from the steamy heat. She used a silk-clad forearm to brush a strand of hair away from her face. Long sleeves in the summertime were impractical no matter how becoming the garment. But she wanted to look her best, and the emerald-green silk clung to her figure in all the right places, besides enlivening the color of her eyes.

Her eyes needed some brightening. They were dull with uncertainty and lack of sleep. Even a letter from her parents, glowing with accounts of their trip, hadn't served to dispel the gloomy mood she'd been in all day.

She had asked for it, she told herself. When she'd told Jake she would take whatever time they had, she had asked for the pain and the heartache.

The strings to her apron got tangled as she tried to undo the knot and she tugged at them distractedly as she glanced at the clock. Six-thirty. She left the kitchen, stopping at the thermostat in the hall to set the air conditioning down a notch and wandered into the study to flip on the television. The audio portion came on immediately but it took a while for the video to warm up.

The news people seemed awfully excited about something she thought with a frown as she watched the blank screen. Slowly the blurred images became definite shapes and she saw a mélange of people moving about. The camera honed in on the angry features of a man shouting something unintelligible and shaking his fist, before moving back for a wider view of the scene. With a growing sense of foreboding Miranda recognized the control tower at the St. Simons airport. Her apron, finally untied, gripped in her hands, she sank to a chair, perching on its edge. Her heart was pounding heavily in her chest, and a ringing in her ears threatened to drown out the sound of the television. She leaned forward in the chair, straining to hear.

The well-known correspondent's voice was agitated, unlike his usual smooth tones. "The pickets have gotten between the president and his helicopter! I can see no weapons, but from the sheer numbers this could develop into a dangerous situation. There must be three hundred or more people here at the small St. Simons airport...."

A placard was waved in front of the camera, temporarily obscuring the view. It read Cut Defense Spending. The man was shoved roughly out of the way and another placard replaced his: Save Our Jobs.

"... most of them from the nearby nuclear submarine base at St. Mary's," the correspondent was saying. "The Secret Service has formed a wedge, a human shield around the president...dammit! Get out of the way!" The camera wavered up toward the sky. There was a loud report. "What was that?" the newsman shouted.

Miranda stood abruptly and switched off the television set. That's enough, she told herself. She moved like an automaton. Her legs were numb as she walked out of the room. I don't want to see; I don't want to know. Jake!

Back in the kitchen she threw the apron on the counter. Then, through glazed, pain-filled eyes, she looked around blindly. Crowds like that were uncontrollable. One person, that would be all it took, one crazy neurotic with a gun....

Oh, God, Jake! No matter how much advance planning.... The president! She shook her head to clear her frantic thoughts. There was something strange, bizarre...something that wasn't right, but she couldn't put her finger on the irregularity.

Then she suddenly remembered. The helicopter carrying the president to Jacksonville was to have left at five o'clock. It was now after six-thirty. Was the footage she just saw on film? Even now he could be ... they could be ....

She whirled and ran back to the study. The television seemed to take even longer to warm up this time. She banged her fist on top of the set impotently.

"The president is all right! I repeat, the president of the United States is unharmed. We have reports that there have been some injuries but the president is safe."

"What injuries?" Miranda pleaded with the television to tell her.

Suddenly the confused sounds, the screams and shouting were replaced by the calm voice of the anchorman on the nightly news. "You have just seen footage from our affiliate in Brunswick, Georgia. We still have no information concerning the other injuries reported during this afternoon's demonstration. We repeat, the president of the United States narrowly escaped injury this afternoon when two groups of demonstrators clashed at the small airport in St. Simons, Georgia. Even as I speak the chief executive is boarding Air Force One in Jacksonville for the return trip to Washington. We will keep you posted when further updates are available. In other stories in the news ...."

Miranda sat as though turned to stone, never taking her eyes from the screen. Pictures blinked at her, to be replaced by others, but they didn't register. Finally the news was over without further reference to the incident.

Still she sat, unable to move except for the twisting and turning of her fingers as she wrung them together. She watched, but did not see, the host of a quiz show introduce the contestants for tonight. Laughter . . . applause . . . .

It took a minute for another, more persistent sound to penetrate the self-protective paralysis. When she finally heard the loud knocking she rose slowly to her feet and crossed the room to the door leading outside. She hesitated. Her face was expressionless. Did she really want to open this door? What if it was Donald? Come to tell her . . . . With a movement that was almost violent she reached for the knob and wrenched it open. Her relief was so overwhelming that she almost fainted.

Jake stood there looking tired but wonderfully, fabulously whole.

She fell into his arms. "I just heard." Her hands sought his face, touching each feature, running the length of his arms. "You're all right!" She grasped his hands, drawing him inside. "Is he really all right, too? Of course he is. You wouldn't be here otherwise. Oh, Jake!" Wrapping her arms around his waist she clung to him. "I was so afraid for you!"

Jake looked over her head to the television, and held her very close. "Sh-h-h, honey. I'm fine," he said, rocking her slightly. "The president's fine. It looked worse than it was."

He consoled the woman in his arms automatically but there was an expression of resigned sadness on his face. This was it. This was the reason he had to leave her, to relinquish forever any residue of hope that things might have worked out. What had she said? "Sometimes weak, often strong." Miranda was strong, but not strong enough, he told himself bitterly. No woman was. It was just too much to expect. He had to leave, now.

"But the reporter said there were injuries. I heard a shot." Her head nodded in the direction of the television. She glared at it accusingly.

"The man exaggerated, honey," he said firmly, smoothing the hair away from her face. He added with a wry smile, "They have a tendency to do that. The crowd got out of control. At one point some people were knocked down but the injuries were minor. I heard a report of a shot but we haven't been able to trace it down."

She looked up at him with a damp smile. "Thank God," she said sincerely. "He's more than just a face on the TV to me now. He knows my parents. He sat in the chair by the pool and talked to me. And you . . . ." Her voice trailed off to a whisper.

He cupped her face in his hand, his thumb stroking the soft line of her cheek. "I understand, sweetheart. I hate the fact that you were worried." Only he knew what the calm facade was costing him. "Demonstrations can be frightening . . . ." He broke off. How would he feel? If he saw Miranda on television in a dangerous situation, how would he react?

Miranda moved her face against his fingers. He lowered his head, blindly seeking her lips. His arms crushed her to him. His hand traced down her spine. What began as a gesture of comfort became an anguished farewell. How could he bear to leave her, this glorious woman, this marvel of femininity? But how could he not? He was afraid to care, afraid to be cared for. His loyalty was to one man. Divided, it would be weakened unacceptably.

The desperation in Jake's kiss finally got through to Miranda, and when he lifted his head she was suddenly afraid to meet his eyes. Her fears were realized the moment she looked into his steady, guarded gaze. She studied his ruggedly handsome face for a minute in silence and took a long shaky breath. "You're leaving."

He nodded.

She shuddered, sickened. The reality that she had so dreaded was at hand. "Tonight?"

"Yes."

She wasn't surprised, she told herself as she moved out of the circle of his arms. The premonition had been alive all along, deep inside her. Somehow she had known that she would not even have this last night with him.

Miranda felt confusion and shock crashing down about her, as though she were being bombarded with all the weapons of hell, but she reached for some inner strength, grabbed it with both hands, and held on tenaciously. "Do you have time for dinner?"

Jake glanced at his watch and then wondered why. He didn't have a plane reservation, would probably spend the night in the Jacksonville airport after he turned in the rental car. He shouldn't stay. "I have an hour."

An hour. One hour and then he would be out of her life forever. Miranda swallowed a sob. "Well, the roast is done. You can fix yourself a drink if you like."

"Better not. I'm driving." He looked down into those beautiful, wide eyes. "Would you rather I left now?" he asked gently. "Would it be easier for you?"

The parody of a smile twisted her features into an expression that pierced his heart and left it bleeding. It was a response he'd never felt before. But then he'd never hurt a woman as much as she was hurting. He didn't ask himself how he knew her feelings so well, but he did.

"Not prolong the agony?" she asked unsteadily.

"Something like that," he admitted. Suddenly realization swept through him like a tide—he loved Miranda, truly loved her with the depth of devotion that poets wrote about. An increase of pressure from somewhere inside his chest made it difficult for him to breathe and left him floundering helplessly in his own emotions. How could he have miscalculated his feelings to such a degree?

"Nonsense," he heard her say. The word seemed to come from a long distance away and echoed, as though it was spoken through a tunnel.

"The food is ready. You ... you may as well have dinner before you start out." She turned with a swirl of green silk around her knees.

He followed her blurred figure into the kitchen, stumbling slightly on the carpet, putting out a hand to catch himself. He had to go! He wanted to stay. Oh, God, how he wanted to stay.

She opened the oven door to check the roast. As he watched with a different kind of hunger from any he'd ever known, she opened a cabinet.

Taking down two plates of her mother's best china, she turned toward the door that led to the dining room.

"Miranda, you have every right to hate me," he choked.

The plates hit the floor, splintering into a million pieces. Miranda was perfectly still for a long moment, not even daring to breathe. If he had plunged a knife between her shoulder blades it could not have hurt any more than the imprudent statement.

She fought against wave after wave of nausea. Finally, slowly, she turned. She knew that her face was a mask, expressionless; and the knowledge was her only support, the only thing to keep her upright. Could she make her voice work one more time? "I have *no* rights where you're concerned," she whispered through frozen lips. "You have gone to a lot of trouble to make that clear. I was just too stupid to give up hoping that you'd change your mind."

He took a step toward her. He didn't know what he would have said, what he would have done, but he was drawn to her with an instinct as old as life.

"No!"

The violence behind the exclamation halted him in his tracks. "Miranda . . . ."

"Get out," she said, very quietly. "Go." When he didn't move she spoke again. Her voice was now a thin weak thread of sound. "If you have any feeling for me, Jake, any feeling at all, please leave."

He could not resist the temptation to drink in the sight of her one last time, a memory to hold forever when his arms were empty. His eyes made the farewell journey down her body to her toes and back up again. When they returned to her face he realized how horribly cruel his self-indulgence had been. "Goodbye, Miranda." His voice faltered slightly on her name.

She didn't answer, wouldn't say goodbye.

He left, pausing just outside the door to blink the moisture from his eyes, to take a long restorative breath. Then he strode determinedly across the lawn. When he reached the coach house he took the steps two at a time. His luggage waited on the floor of the bedroom.

Grabbing for the two cases, he retraced his steps as though the hounds of hell were after him. Not until he was in the car, traveling at a ridiculous speed on the causeway over the marsh did he ask himself how in God's name he was going to get through the rest of his life.

10

A WEEK LATER Miranda stood in front of the mirror in her bedroom and delivered a stern lecture to herself. "Wash your hair, put on some makeup." She leaned closer to her reflection and corrected, "A lot of makeup, and plaster a smile on your face. Three weeks may have changed your life forever, but they didn't end it, you fool."

The telephone rang on the bedside table. Miranda groaned, knowing instantly who was on the other end of the line. Determinedly she crossed the room and picked up the receiver. "Good morning, Patty," she said, deliberately using the diminutive that she knew her friend hated.

"You must be feeling better," Patricia commented wryly.

Patricia's daily phone calls were made out of friendship and love, and Miranda appreciated her friend's concern. But sometimes she wanted to be left alone. She sighed and sat on the edge of the bed. "I am feeling better, Patricia. Thanks."

"You don't have to sigh like that. I know I've been a pest." The voice on the phone was tight.

Now she'd hurt her dearest friend, and that

was the last thing she'd wanted to do. Miranda smiled with effort into the telephone. The feeling was unfamiliar, a taut pinching sensation in her cheeks. She realized it was the first time she'd smiled in a week. "Don't be offended," she begged. "You've been so thoughtful to call. I'm the one who's a pest."

It was Patricia's turn to sigh. "If you'd just get *mad*, Miranda," she urged, and sighed again. "What I wouldn't give to see your redheaded temper erupt."

Miranda had to laugh at that. "You make me sound like a shrew."

Patricia chuckled. "You can be rather formidable. Luckily it doesn't happen often."

"Would you like to bring the children over to swim?" Miranda asked hastily. She didn't want to remember the last time her temper had gotten away from the control she placed so rigidly on it—the night she'd arrived on the island.

"Can't. Dan has a three-day medical meeting in Atlanta and he's taking me along. We're leaving after lunch."

Miranda realized suddenly that she would miss her friend's support. "Well, don't worry about me. I have a dinner date tonight."

"A dinner date!" squealed Patricia.

"With Donald. He bullied me."

"Good for him," said Patricia firmly. "Have a nice time, and I'll call you when I get back."

"You have a nice time, too. Bye." Miranda replaced the receiver with an affectionate smile on her lips. She wasn't alone; she had good friends and neighbors who cared about her. This other void would never go away but it could be filled with friendship, if not love.

Donald Webster had telephoned a few minutes before Patricia had, to invite her to dine with him at The Cloister. She had attempted to put him off, but he was insistent. "I haven't seen you on the beach or at the pool for a week. What are you doing shut up in that house, Miranda?"

She had murmured some feeble excuse about work, which he'd dismissed immediately. "I knew that something was bothering you when you had dinner here last week. I would be remiss in my friendship for your parents if I didn't try to help."

The childless widower had known her for years and his concern was genuine. "Donald, please. It isn't a subject I can discuss quite yet. Maybe later," she responded.

"Very well, my dear, I won't pry, but you must go with me to the hotel tonight so I can see for myself that you are all right."

She'd hesitated.

"Otherwise I might have to mention the situation to your parents in my next letter. As a matter of fact, I believe I owe them one."

He was an avid correspondent, and she didn't doubt he meant every word he said. "Donald!" she admonished with an unwilling smile. "That's blackmail."

"Of course. Will you go with me?"

"Of course," she mocked affectionately. "I'll come through the gate. What time?"

"Seven o'clock sharp."

"Naturally." The unwilling smile became a grin. Donald was a retired military man and seven o'clock *meant* sharp. Suddenly she felt a little better.

Making something presentable out of the wreck she'd become took all day and wasn't easy. Permanent lines of misery seemed to have sprouted between her brows. She tried to scrub them away, but just one fleeting thought of Jake and they reappeared as though by magic. Her skin had all the glow of tallow, and her cheekbones stood out in sharp relief against the shadows under her eyes.

Still, that evening, when she had dressed in a smart little black beaded cocktail dress, and applied color to her lips with a heavy hand, her spirits rose slightly. The look was...interesting. She turned slightly aside from the mirror.

Tragedy added a certain helpless appeal to her features that she might be able to copy for the next production of "Camille." She threw her hairbrush across the room in an excess of self-disgust and hurried downstairs. Damn Jake Stewart! He was *not* going to ruin her life!

People didn't waste away from unrequited love these days...did they? She had already decided that the cure for her malaise was work. As soon as her parents returned from Europe she would go back to Athens.

Her department head would be pleased. He had tried to talk her into staying for summer school. It was too late to teach a class in the long session, but there was a short session beginning the second week in July and she intended to be there. The glorious lazy summer that she'd looked forward to was ruined. The best remedy for her now was to fill her days to the point of exhaustion in hope that the nights would be halfway bearable.

Gathering up a black-lace mantilla, to cover her bare shoulders, and a tiny clutch bag, she left the house.

"I'm glad you decided to come, Miranda," Donald said a short while later.

They strolled through the fading light in the direction of the hotel. Her hand was tucked in the crook of his elbow, and she felt protected, almost as comforted as if it had been her own father.

No cars were on the road; no exhaust fumes overpowered the floral fragrances of jasmine and hibiscus; no noisy engines drowned out the songs of crickets. They passed the tennis courts, empty now. Guests of the hotel would be inside, dressing for one of Sea Island's sumptuous meals. The island had returned to its conventional tranquility. It had endured the visit of a president, as it had endured the visits of other noteworthy persons, with no visible effects.

"Did I have a choice?" she asked, looking with a smile. Donald Webster was almost as handsome as her own father. With his shock of silver hair and his military bearing, he looked much younger than the sixty-eight she knew him to be.

He patted her hand. "It's for your own good."

She laughed. "Stock answer for a bully," she accused.

He became very serious. "Did I really bully you, Miranda?"

She looked down. The pavement moved beneath their feet, his highly polished shoes and her black silk pumps. When she met his gaze it was with a tremulous smile. "It *was* for my own good."

"I haven't seen that expression of sadness in your eyes in many years, my dear. Would you like to tell me what, or who, put it there?"

"Perhaps. Someday." She gave a soft sigh. "Right now it's too close."

Miranda did not realize just how close the source of her misery was.

They climbed the wide shallow steps of the Spanish-style entrance to The Cloister. The lobby was large and square. In the center resting on an authentic Duncan Fyfe dining table was a huge Flemish arrangement of long-stemmed fresh flowers. The hardwood floors were softened with Oriental rugs.

A photographer was stationed in the lobby to snap family-group pictures using the flowers as a background. The giggles of organdy-clad little girls quite drowned out the complaints of scrubbed, brushed and jacketed little boys. Later the prints would be displayed prominently as the guests left the dining room.

"I've always wondered how he gets those things developed so fast," murmured Donald, as the man clicked his shutter, preserving the image of a family of five.

"He has to so they'll be ready for you to order copies. Mother has dozens of them." Miranda didn't want her picture taken. She started to shake her head as the photographer directed them to the table, but Donald was guiding her to the spot.

"Please, my dear. Think what it will do for my image, having my picture taken with a beautiful young woman." He smiled and she shrugged.

The flash went off, temporarily blinding them. Miranda blinked, trying to rid her vision of silver streaks and spots. Then she had to blink again, because she couldn't believe the message her eyes were sending to her brain. It couldn't be! With her knees threatening to collapse, she grabbed for something, anything to keep her upright, and caught a handful of Donald's coat sleeve. Surely she was dreaming. Either that or she had lost her mind.

"Hello, Miranda." Jake's deep husky voice brought her back to earth. It *was* him. And he looked magnificent in a midnight-blue tuxedo, his shoulders as broad as forever, his smile loving and oh so very welcome.

Miranda's mouth curved into the loveliest smile Jake had ever seen as she took a step toward him with her hand outstretched. She moved hesitantly, like a sleepwalker, but with grace and elegance.

Jake had to swallow past the lump in his throat and fight an overpowering urge to crush her in his arms. He took her hand in a grip of iron, threatening the fragile bones for a moment before he recalled himself.

"Oh, my darling," he breathed for her ears alone. Vaguely he registered the flash of light that went off somewhere to his left, but lightning could have struck beside him at this moment, and he wouldn't have flinched. Her other hand came up, and he grabbed for it like a drowning man reaching for a lifeline. He searched her eyes, finding a matching wonder in her expression which reflected his.

That was all they could do, here in this public place. He could have given her a discreet kiss, like friends meeting socially, but he knew instinctively that when his lips met hers, it would not be a discreet kiss. If he ever got his arms around this woman it would be a long, long time, if ever, before he would be able to let go.

A restless movement and a beaming smile over Jake's shoulder drew Miranda's attention. Confusion swept up to color her face. Suddenly she remembered where she was, who was holding her hands. *Oh, no. I'll have to go through it all over again,* she thought in dismay.

"Are you going to introduce us, son?" The man fairly beamed at Miranda.

Jake seemed to be having some trouble mastering his feelings, too. Reluctantly he released one of Miranda's hands, keeping a firm hold on the other one. "Miranda, I'd like you to meet my dad, Taylor Rutledge. Dad, this is Miranda Woodbarry," he said as though he were presenting the crown jewels for his stepfather's inspection. "And this is Donald Webster," he added.

The two older men shook hands before Taylor Rutledge turned back to her. "So you are Miranda?"

Her disconcerted senses were beginning to untangle and a thousand questions hovered on her lips, but her good manners finally asserted themselves. "How do you do, Mr. Rutledge?"

If her voice was shaky he pretended not to notice. His smile was warm as he took the offered hand. "This is a pleasure I've looked forward to for a long time," he said ambiguously.

His words brought her startled gaze to meet the twinkle in his. Something wasn't right here. She returned the smile automatically, struggling to clarify this whole unbelievable situation in her befuddled mind. It would help if Jake were to release her left hand. She wiggled her fingers tentatively, but he refused to take the hint.

Jake's stepfather was a total surprise. The tall slender man fairly oozed self-confidence and charm. He wore his beautifully tailored black tuxedo as though it were his everyday habit. Her bewildered eyes switched to Jake's and back again to the debonair older man. Where had she gotten the impression that he was lonely, retired with limited means? Obviously that was a gigantic misconception.

Frowning, she tried to remember. Hadn't Jake used their differing backgrounds as an excuse for not getting involved? He had let her believe that her family's wealth was a major stumbling block. Why would he do that? And why had she accepted it so easily? Because she had been too sensitive to the idea ever since Charles.

"You are from Detroit?" she asked Taylor Rutledge. The words weren't merely social conversation. She wanted to hear him confirm that he was who Jake said he was.

"That's right," he told her. "This is my first visit to Sea Island in many years. My first wife and I honeymooned here."

Even his voice was a contradiction. The tones were cultured, refined. She gave him a grateful smile for the extra seconds his casual observation afforded. Suspicion had planted a seed in her brain which flowered into irritation.

Jake had deliberately misled her. It was clear that their backgrounds weren't dissimilar at all. Miranda didn't like to be misled—even now she couldn't call it a lie. Jake's honesty was not in question, just his motives.

Her eyes took on a glittering chill as she threw a look at Jake. "And what do you do there, Mr. Rutledge?" She didn't really care what he did but his answer stunned her.

Taylor Rutledge wasn't offended. On the contrary, he seemed pleased by her interest. "My company makes the padding that goes into cars."

"Padding?" Donald asked the question for her.

He chuckled. "Not very glamorous I'm afraid, and totally invisible. The padding under the carpet, the dashboard, the armrests, the doors." He shrugged. "And we make some manufacturing equipment for the automakers. I've been trying to get Jake into the business for years."

"You have?"

His smile was one of satisfaction. "Now, it seems, I am about to succeed."

She didn't ask him to explain. She was very impatient to get Mr. Jake Stewart alone to demand a few explanations, such as why he had come back to Sea Island. She had gone through the most hellish week of her life because of him and she didn't want to repeat the experience.

Jake was impatient to get her alone, too, but his reasons were different. When Miranda asked for a moment to speak to him alone, he squeezed her hand in response. Her glare surprised him into releasing her fingers but he murmured, "Excuse us," to the two men and hurried to catch up as she stalked down a long stone-floored corridor toward the solarium.

The huge room was deserted except for the tropical birds in a ceiling-high cage in the corner. They flitted around for a moment at the unexpected intrusion, then settled down again.

Miranda walked to the center of the room, then whirled to face him. "Why are you here?" she demanded. Her words echoed off the plastered walls and stone floor.

Jake wasn't sure what had sparked her temper, but he wasn't about to do anything to fuel it. If he tried to take her in his arms right now, much as he ached to, she was liable to punch him with one of those clenched fists. His love was a formidable woman when angered, he acknowledged with affection. Still, the sight of her soft shoulders, the contours of her breasts in that sexy dress, her small waist, set up a stirring in his loins, a hunger to taste her mouth, to hold her, to make long, slow love to her.

No, not yet. He unbuttoned the tux jacket and shoved his hands into the pockets. This called for diplomacy. "I'm here because I couldn't stay away, Miranda. I want to marry you." Diplomacy? He heard the harshness in his own voice and chided himself for a lack of it.

Her jaw fell in an expression of stunned disbelief. He really couldn't fault her response, he thought, running a restless hand through his hair. This was no way to propose. He sounded more like an antagonist than a lover. Foolishly he tried to rectify the mistake with words when action would have been more effective. "I'm going to resign from the Secret Service," he told her hastily.

"Wha-at?" She drew the word out, her beautiful green eyes widening first, then narrowing. Her fists came up to sit on her hips. "Why on earth would you want to do that?"

"Why the hell do you think?" he blurted, angry at being put on the defensive. Then he filled his lungs with air and slowly let it out. The warning signs were out. A storm was fast approaching. If he weren't very careful he could end up on a reef. "So we can get married," he continued in a calmer tone. "Taylor told you. He has no children of his own. He's been after me for years to go into the business with him."

"Why did you deceive me? You let me think he was a lonely old man, living on a pension."

"I thought it would be easier to let you think we had a social class difference than trying to explain my feelings about marriage. I apologize."

"And what *are* your feelings about marriage?"

"I can't be married and keep my job," Jake responded flatly.

She folded her arms just underneath her breasts, bringing his attention to their beautiful shape. "There's no rule that Secret Service agents have to be single. I'm aware of that," she stated sarcastically. "So...let me see...what could your reasoning possibly be?" One hand cupped her elbow. A rosy tipped finger tapped against her cheek in mock speculation while the rest of her fingers curled into her palm. "There are no restrictions on you, so the fault must lie with me," she finished.

Jake wrenched his gaze from the top of her dress and wiped his damp forehead with the back of his hand. This wasn't going well at all! "Miranda . . . darling, could we sit down and discuss this thing rationally," he pleaded.

"I'm perfectly rational," she told him coolly, replacing her arm in its original resistive position.

"Well, dammit, I'm not! Sit down!" His explosive exclamation startled the birds and they fluttered restlessly again.

She sat, in a straight-backed chair, her spine rigid, putting an end to his hope that if he could sit beside her, take her in his arms, this nightmare might come to an end.

He took another chair, sat in it facing her and leaned forward, his forearms resting on his knees. "I'll try to explain. I had a good friend. His name was Harry."

"You explained about him."

Had he? He couldn't remember. He went on. "His wife . . . well, if she heard a rumor, a news story, she went wild with fear. It didn't take much to set her off. It's hard on a woman, this life, hard on a marriage." He paused, letting his gaze drop to his clasped hands.

Before he could go on, Miranda interrupted. "You don't think I'm capable of handling it?"

"I don't think any woman is capable of handling it," he said bluntly.

If he had waved a red flag at the largest bull in Spain, he couldn't have set off more fury. She stood abruptly. A vein in her neck throbbed beneath the surface of her skin. "How dare you insult me so," she bit out through clenched teeth. She had to stop for a long calming breath. "How dare you judge me, and my strength, so arbitrarily. I am not flattered by your sacrifice, Jake, or by your assumption that I can't stand up under trouble or adversity. I am no coward.

"This has been the worst week of my life." She had to pause again, then she clasped her hands together at her waist and her chin came up in defiance. "But I am *not* falling apart."

He forced himself to remain seated. What he wanted to do was shake her until her teeth rattled. Why was she being so damned obstinate? And how the hell could a marriage proposal be taken as an insult? He knew that he was presenting his case poorly but she was throwing him off balance, just as she had been doing since their first encounter. He raked agitated fingers through his hair again, leaving it disordered. "Harry's wife met him at the door practically every night with recriminations and tears. A week ago you met me at the door, upset by a television news program."

"I didn't cry," she defended herself heatedly.

"Yes, you did, Miranda!" he snapped.

"Dammit! I did not! You've seen me cry. The night you pulled me out of the window I cried." She swept the air between them in a broad gesture. "But a week ago I *did not* cry."

He screened his expression. His elbow rested on his knee while he stroked his chin with thumb and forefinger, but he didn't answer because he was at a loss; he didn't know what to say. He remembered the childlike tears she had shed, with her cheek pressed against the side of the house. No, she hadn't cried like that a week ago.

"Worry isn't a sign of weakness, but of caring, Jake." Her voice was calmer and he looked up hopefully. But she went on before he could speak. "What a shame you never learned that lesson. I think it's you who are the coward—an emotional coward."

His head jerked at the accusation. No one had ever accused him of cowardice before. He surged to his feet and planted himself directly in front of her. "You're crazy!"

"And you're defensive!"

Jake searched her face, seeking an explanation that wasn't there. Confused, he shook his head, and his shoulders slumped in a gesture of defeat. "Why are we arguing like this, Miranda?" he whispered. "I love you!"

"Do you, Jake?" Her voice was quiet now, and infinitely sad. "If you loved me you would know me better." Her fingers tightened, whitening her knuckles. "You'd know that I would refuse to be responsible for your giving up a job that you love and believe in." She turned to go.

"Miranda . . . ." He choked on her name, halting her for a moment.

She shook her head, sending her glorious hair flying about her shoulders. She seemed to be shaking him off at the same time. "I won't accept your sacrifice."

JAKE LOOKED ACROSS THE DINNER TABLE at his step-father with pain-filled eyes. "You wouldn't believe it, Dad. I made such a *mess* of everything." The words were wrung from him.

Taylor leaned back in his chair, one forearm resting on the white cloth, and curled his fingers around his glass. The soft light of the chandelier above his head picked out the silver streaks in his sandy-brown hair but shadowed the amused sadness in his eyes. He regarded his son—for Jake was his son in every way but biologically—with a steady, sympathetic gaze.

He had hoped that his own problems were solved. Ostensibly retired, he continued to be active in the decision-making process of his company. But he wasn't satisfied with the situation. The company needed new, young ideas. He would turn the whole thing over to Jake in a minute, lock, stock and barrel, with the utmost confidence.

"Do you want to talk about it, son?"

"You know how I feel. The Service is rough on any kind of relationship, particularly marriage." Jake took a long pull on his Scotch and sighed. "I tried to explain that to Miranda when I told her I was going to quit, but she is so damn bullheaded. She said I had insulted her."

Taylor hid a smile behind his hand. He had always known that someday Jake would meet someone who matched him for strength. He also knew Jake's feelings about marriage and the Secret Service, so he had anticipated the day, hoping Jake would decide to come home. Now the two sentiments were at war with each other. Though he himself would be a loser, he couldn't help enjoying the show. "Your Miranda sounds like a strong, if stubborn, woman."

Jake's face took on the conviction of a man who believes he is right. "No woman is that strong."

Taylor straightened and shook out his napkin as the white-gloved waiter placed his appetizer before him. He was silent while the man moved quietly around the table, then he looked up, ready to resume the conversation. But at the expression of longing on his son's face he swiveled his head to follow the direction of Jake's gaze, sure of what he would see.

Miranda and Donald Webster were seated at a nearby table. The beautiful woman was calm and composed as she conversed with her dinner partner.

Wisely, Taylor chose not to speak for a moment. "Jake," he said at last.

"Sir?" The younger man brought his attention back from the glass he was holding.

"You haven't asked for my advice."

"You know it's welcome, Dad." Jake tried to grin. "Any advice would be welcome at this point." His gaze strayed to Miranda once again, but she was ignoring his scrutiny as though she was totally oblivious to his presence.

A waiter approached to offer her a roll. She shook her head, and the action moved her glorious hair across her bare shoulders. His fingers curled, remembering its silky texture and the way it clung to his hands. "Isn't she the most incredible woman?" he asked.

Taylor chuckled. "Yes, son," he agreed indulgently. "She is very lovely."

Jake laughed softly at himself. "I'm acting like a lovesick adolescent, while she doesn't seem to have a care in the world."

"You don't believe that."

"No. I realize she's hurting, too," he said in a low voice. It was true. No matter how indifferent she appeared he could see the stiffness in the way she held her neck, the defensive way she squared her shoulders. "I just don't know how to heal her hurt when she won't listen to me."

"Have you tried listening to her?"

Jake raised his brows.

"Forgive me for preaching, Jake, but you've made a rather broad assumption based on one tragic experience. Maybe you've been protecting other people for too long. Maybe you don't give them a chance to stand on their own feet. From what you've told me about Miranda, I would say she's capable of handling almost anything without bitterness or recrimination," Taylor commented impassively. "In that way she reminds me of your mother."

Jake looked at him. Slowly, painfully, comprehension dawned. He finally heard what Miranda was saying to him, had been saying all along. Her lack of bitterness over her divorce, her shock at the sight of guns on Sea Island — not fear but shock — and, most achingly, her willingness to take whatever they were granted, for however long—all these things were characteristic of her strength and her love. She had tried to show him but he'd been too damned blind to see.

He caught his breath for a moment before letting it out in a slow stream. The burden of depression he had carried for the last week suddenly grew lighter. "Mother was a strong woman, wasn't she?" he observed in a quiet voice, rife with melancholy.

"As only a tender, loving woman, secure in her femininity, can be." The two men stared at each other, remembering the person they both missed so deeply.

Jake gave a husky chuckle. "I don't know whether she'll forgive me. Miranda has a redhead's temper."

"So did Janice, even without the red hair."

Despite his own misgivings Jake realized at last that the only way he would get his beloved Miranda back would be to stay in his job. As he looked up the decision was in his expression, and so was the apology. "Dad. I'm sorry."

"That's all right, son. I think I knew all along how this would turn out."

"The company...."

"I've had an offer for the company." Taylor leaned back in his chair. "But I believe I'll hang on to it for a while. You may change your mind, or she may, when you have a child. Maybe you'll want to move to Detroit then."

At the thought of Miranda carrying his child, Jake's gaze swung to the table across the room. It was empty. Involuntarily he started to rise, but was stopped by his stepfather's voice. "They left about three minutes ago. Give her time to get home and calm herself. Maybe she'll slip into something comfortable."

Jake laughed and sank back in the chair. "Why you old reprobate," he accused.

"Just being practical," Taylor corrected with a grin. "Shall we have dessert?"

11

"I PRESUME JAKE STEWART is the source of your unhappiness," Donald stated as they walked back home. His voice was quiet but concerned.

Darkness had descended during dinner. The moon had dissolved to nothing in its monthly phase, leaving only the stars in the inky sky.

Miranda, clutching the small black purse to her breast, looked up at the heavens and blinked to clear her vision. The lace shawl covered her shoulders but did very little to protect her from the coldness she felt inside. "Yes, he is."

"He was here with the president."

She nodded. "He's a Secret Service agent, in charge of communications. Actually he came down earlier," she said huskily.

"The group who stayed in the coach house?"

"Yes."

They made their way from the pool of light under one street lamp to another before he spoke again. "You haven't known him for very long."

"No." *Not long at all, and yet it feels like I've known him all my life.* She prepared herself for the lecture she was sure would follow.

Donald sighed. "Well, I suppose it only takes

one sip of wine to tell if you have a good bottle."

Proud that the laugh which escaped didn't sound as hysterical as she felt, she stopped to give Donald a warm hug.

As soon as she'd left Jake in the solarium, Miranda's indignation had evaporated, making room in her heart for the first wave of anguish. She had negotiated the long corridor almost in a stupor, while the wave had quickly become a floodtide, threatening to drown her in its wake. More than anything in the world at that particular moment she had wanted to run from the hotel, from the smiling people around her, from life, from herself.

Donald had said goodbye to Taylor Rutledge and had guided her to the dining room with a hand at her elbow, unaware of her despair. Or so she thought, until now.

She blessed him for being the soul of discretion and kindness that he was and for not having mentioned the subject during dinner. Her feigned composure would probably have broken into a million little pieces, embarrassing poor Donald frightfully.

When they reached her door he said good night in his endearing courtly way.

"Good night, Donald, and thank you."

"Are you sure you're all right, my dear? I don't like to leave you alone. If only your parents were here."

"I'm a big girl now, Donald," she chided gently.

He looked at her with an expression that clearly said the thought hadn't occurred to him, and she hugged him again. "If I need you, I'll call. May I?"

The question seemed to reassure him. "Certainly, Miranda. Anytime."

Miranda watched from the back step as the military-straight shoulders disappeared through the gate in the hedge. The intensity of her emotions, which had held her together during dinner, ebbed away. She had never felt so exhausted, so drained, in all her span of existence.

Leaning heavily against the door frame she shook her head once and opened the clasp of her small clutch bag. Her fingers delved inside, hesitated, then poked about again.

Panic clogged her throat. No! Fate could not be so cruel. Not tonight, when she could barely stand. The shawl fell to the ground as she sank to the top step and dumped the contents of the bag on the concrete beside her. Her eyes were flooding quickly but she could see enough to know that there was no key among the paraphernalia she stirred with her finger. Almost out of her wits, she thought, *this has become a first-rate melodrama.*

Her arms circled her knees and she dropped her head on them. A harsh whimper ripped from her throat. Then another. All at once she was crying in great convulsive sobs, her slender body shuddering from their severity.

How long she wept she didn't know but suddenly she was lifted and cradled against a massive chest in a tender but determined embrace. There was no need to check the identification of the man who held her. A frantic heartbeat shook the white shirtfront beneath her cheek. "Now I'm crying!" she explained frantically. "You see? *Now* I'm crying."

"Oh, my darling! So am I!"

She caught her breath and lifted her wet face. Not Jake, she thought, her eyes wide and unbelieving. But it was true. Tears ran unashamedly in rivulets from his pain-filled eyes to the corners of his mouth.

She reached up to touch them. Dazed and bewildered she assured him, "I'm only crying because I'm locked out again." She was afraid, afraid that she had hurt him too deeply, too permanently, afraid that he would take his arms away.

He gave a choked laugh and buried his face in the soft skin of her neck, bringing her closer into his arms as though he would never release her. "My love, I'm crying because I thought I had lost you forever," he whispered.

Lost her? What was he talking about? He was her world, her existence. Didn't he realize? Her arms wound around his neck tightly. She couldn't bear to see him cry like this. His pain hurt worse—oh, so much worse—than her own. "I love you. I love you," she said over and over so he would know.

"And I love you, my darling." His voice was muffled, but the words were pronounced emphatically, as though he defied anyone, anywhere, to dispute them. He lifted his head to crush her tender, willing lips under his, his hunger profound and intense. He kissed her again and again, until finally he sighed, a long, desperate sound, and brought her once more into the protective embrace under his chin.

"Oh, Jake. I've been so miserable," she cried softly.

"No more, honey. Never again. I need you. I need your strength. You were right—I was a damn coward." His broken phrases were punctuated with more kisses, with caring, tender caresses.

"No! You're the bravest man I know. I'm sorry I said all those terrible things." She nestled against his heartbeat, drawing strength from the sound, from the vitality of his presence.

Slowly joy, like honey, like molasses in the spring, began to spread throughout her body with healing warmth, revitalizing, energizing. She stroked his dark head, his broad back, his shoulders. And then she held him, simply held him, until the height and magnitude of their emotions descended to a more controllable plane.

When they finally drew apart, their eyes met. They each gave a small laugh. Perched securely on his lap, she dried his tears with her hands; he dried hers; and their fingers lingered to explore each other's features. In an excess of sensitivity Miranda threw her arms around his neck again, to be crushed to his chest.

After a minute more she became aware that desire was quickly taking the place of tenderness and concern. His hand, sliding up and down her back from bare skin to beaded fabric was beginning to do wonderful things to her. "Darling?"

"Um-m-m?" His tongue traced the shape of her ear, and he blew softly into it, setting off even more delightful shivers.

"We're locked out."

"I remember," he said huskily, covering her mouth in another hungry kiss. His tongue sought the sweetness inside her mouth, moving greedily over her teeth and beyond to play a sensual game with hers.

It was a long, lingering kiss. When he finally raised his head he heaved a heavy sigh and smiled down at her. His fingers tucked a strand of hair behind her ear and lingered at the side of her neck. "It won't be easy for me to wait while we clean up all that glass. I don't suppose . . . the beach?" he asked, teasing hopefully.

Miranda laughed in open relief and delight. Jake, the real Jake whom she loved so profoundly, was back. He helped her to her feet, keeping her under one arm. The expression in his eyes was still raw, belying the light words. He was quickly regaining the self-confidence that characterized his nature.

"No, not the beach," she informed him gently, looking up at him through her lashes. "You said once that a nice comfortable bed was the best place to make love. I want a bed where we can spend the whole night loving each other."

Jake couldn't resist her sweet words or her allure. His hand grasped the back of her head to bring her against his length. "You are a provocative wench, and cruel, too. The beach is very comfortable."

She arched into the hardness of his body. Her fingers worked their way under his dinner jacket around to his back and slid over his hips. "As comfortable as my bed?"

He groaned. His hand splayed at the small of her back to move her against his arousal. "Definitely cruel," he accused hoarsely and stepped back. He gripped her shoulders as he looked around helplessly.

She read his mind. "What are we going to use to break the window, Jake?" she asked, her eyes glimmering. "My purse is too small."

"Stay here. I'll see what I can find." He plunged his hands into his pockets and, taking long, impatient strides, disappeared around a corner of the house.

Miranda sat back down on the step, content—no, grateful—to let him take charge. She was barely able to think, much less act. While she waited she picked up the contents of her purse.

Jake was back in moments but inside of the house. The light from the kitchen spilled out the window, startling Miranda. He opened the door behind her. "I can tell I'm going to have to teach you something about security, my love," he growled as he reached down a hand to haul her to her feet.

She grabbed for her purse and shawl. "Was the house unlocked?" she asked, and then realized how stupid the question was. She smiled appealingly as he pulled her through the door and locked it after them.

"Yes," he answered gruffly. "Now, before we go any further—" He broke off what he'd been about to say. Miranda had tossed her purse and shawl on the countertop and was tugging one end of his black tie free.

"Go on. I'm listening," she said as she began to work the studs from their holes.

"I'm not going to quit my job, Miranda, not yet."

That got her attention. She raised her head to peer at him through her thick lashes. "Does that mean I'm on trial?" she asked with sudden misgiving.

"No, it doesn't mean that at all, honey," Jake answered solemnly. He cupped her face to bring it back into the curve of his neck and wrapped her in his arms. "It means that we're going to compromise."

She nuzzled her face into his throat. "What kind of compromise?"

"I'll stay on with the Service until you get pregnant. Then I'm definitely leaving. And I want no argument from you."

"Okay." Pregnant. What a wonderful idea. She would look like a big pumpkin, she'd be

clumsy and cross, and she'd love every minute
of it. There would have to be compromises
over her job, too. But they could discuss them
at another time. Luckily there were theater
groups all over the country . . . maybe even in
Detroit.

"You won't get an argument. I can compromise, too." That idea led to another. She leaned
back in his arms and again set to work on the
studs in his shirt. Her lips were curved in a
playful smile but her hands were trembling
slightly. "Jake?"

"Um-m-m?" He sounded distracted. One long
finger delved into the neckline of her dress to
stroke lightly over a hard nipple.

She gasped at the sensation. "Did you by any
chance do any 'advance plananing' for tonight?" she asked in a weak voice.

Instead of answering her question or stopping
her progress with the studs, he backed up to sit
on the table edge and pulled her between his
outstretched legs. His hands on her hips guided
her against him, making her overwhelmingly
aware of just how distracted he was.

"You want to get me pregnant right quick,
don't you?" she accused unsteadily.

"Honey, what I want to do to you right quick
is much more fundamental than that. You feel
so good against me, sweetheart," he murmured.
His head had fallen forward and his lips nib-
bled hungrily at her bare shoulder.

Finally she finished with the last of the pesky
studs and dropped them on the table beside

him. She plucked at the fine fabric of his shirt, pushing the sides apart to reveal his virile chest. Leaning forward she inhaled the wonderful masculine smell of him, and her lips left a soft kiss. Her nails raked through the wiry curling hair there to find his flat nipples. He groaned from deep in his throat, pulling her roughly against him. "Miranda, love, you're killing me. Let's go upstairs."

"Yes," she said breathlessly, winding her arms around his neck. "I've never understood why we seem to play so many love scenes in the kitchen.

He had already slid an arm under her knees to lift her in his arms and was headed for the stairway.

They stood in the faint light spilling into the bedroom from the hall and undressed each other. When all their clothes had been discarded his fingers began an unhurried, renewed exploration of her body, reviving emotions she'd never thought to feel again.

As usual his thoughts ran parallel to hers. "You are so beautiful, my darling. I was afraid I would never see you, touch you, like this again."

He shaped and stroked her breasts to fill his hands, slid his long beautiful fingers between her thighs to tease the warm moistness of her femininity, and finally fit her hips to the hard planes of his masculine body.

Her own hands traced the wide musculature of his chest, wound around his back, reveling in the smooth skin under her fingers, before coming up to bury themselves in his hair.

At last he could stand no more. He whipped aside the spread and fell backward on the bed, taking her with him.

Her fingers curled hungrily into the muscles of his shoulders, her hair forming a blazing, wild-flower-scented curtain about their heads, filtering the light to enclose their kisses in a cocoon of seclusion. She shifted one leg to run her toes up his calf and her breasts scraped sensually across his hair-roughened chest, provoking an instantaneous, hungry sound of need. Suddenly she found herself on her back staring up into the dark beauty of his eyes.

His soft possessive smile filled her with a cherished warmth as his fingers threaded into her hair. "I love you, Miranda, with everything I am," he whispered as he slowly filled her emptiness, her aching need, with a physical vow equally as strong as the tender devotion of the spoken words.

"And I love you . . . forever," she answered as she received him with a tender welcome.

Their loving was magical, rhythmic, building in intensity until they were transported, clinging together, into a realm of mysterious enchantment completely different from any other. Her eyes, which had begun to close, opened wide to take in every nuance of the wealth of this feeling, of this rapture.

The mystic knowledge of love and its sorcery had wiped away all vestiges of hesitation from

both of them and had seasoned their joining
with a passion that flamed out of control, taking
them both by surprise.

The wonder in her eyes was mirrored in his
own. He smoothed the hair away from her face
in tender concern. His fingers remained to
cradle her cheek. "Miranda! I've never known
anything like that in my life," he whispered in
awe, still shaking with the force of the magic.

"I-I'm glad you were with me," she answered
shakily, turning her face into the palm of his
hand.

He moved to one side, gathering her into the
circle of his arms with a possessiveness she
didn't mind at all. "I'll always be with you, my
darling," he promised. His hands wandered
softly, soothingly over her skin, stroking her
shoulder, her back, the dip of her waist.

Miranda closed her eyes and was gradually
drawn into sweet, fulfilling sleep. A floating
cloud of happiness was her mattress; her blanket, the heavenly embrace of her love.

The night was too short for their physical desire to be even partially slaked, but long enough
for them to seal their commitment to each other
for the rest of their lives. They talked and made
love, dozed and talked. With the first light of
dawn they were awake, filled with unexpected
energy and the joy of life.

At what Miranda considered a decent hour,
Jake called his stepfather and invited him for
breakfast. Then she called to invite Donald.

"I feel terribly guilty about Taylor. After all,

he thought this was to be your vacation together," she told Jake. "And you walk out on him the first night."

"I have an idea he understands," he answered wryly. Then he snapped his fingers. "Hey! I lost something in your driveway last night." Hurriedly he got out of the tumbled bed and reached for his trousers. "I hope it's still there."

Miranda propped on her elbows and looked at him bewilderedly. "What is it?" she asked.

"Surprise," he answered as he disappeared.

She was in the shower when he returned a few minutes later.

He joined her there but refused to disclose the surprise. "It isn't waterproof," he told her with a grin and reached for the soap.

Jake followed her into the bedroom, watching and wondering if Miranda would see the same thing he saw. She spied it immediately, propped against the mirror of the dresser. The picture of them had been snapped last night in that first instant of reunion. The smile on her face was filled with all the love she'd tried to hide later in the solarium. And the yearning in his was quite obvious.

"That was what gave me the courage to come to you again," he said huskily from behind her. He wrapped his arms around her towel-clad waist. "When I heard you crying I started to run. I must have dropped it. It was halfway down the block," he laughed softly, but he knew the expression in his eyes was completely serious. "I promise never to cause you tears again, my love."

She turned in his arms and reached for him, and Jake thought he'd never felt such exultation in his life.

It was almost time for Taylor and Donald to join them for breakfast when they finally descended the stairs arm in arm.

"Do you have a passport?" Jake asked as they entered the kitchen.

"You're full of surprises this morning." Miranda smiled up at him, puzzled. "Yes, I do. Why? Are we going somewhere?"

"Where are your parents?" He turned her in his arms and looped his hands behind her back.

"They're in Paris—" she leaned forward to kiss his chin "—or Rome or somewhere. Why?" she repeated softly.

"Because I know you'll want them at our wedding," he threw out casually. "I have two weeks of vacation left, darling. I was thinking we might hop on a plane tomorrow—we'd have to take Taylor. I hope you don't mind."

He had her full attention now. "No, I don't mind," she said weakly. "I like him very much."

"And we'd get married in Rome or Paris or wherever. We could spend our honeymoon on the Riviera or Portugal or somewhere." He grinned. "I presume you do have their itinerary."

She nodded.

"What do you think?"

Her hands rested lightly against the front of his shirt. "I think you're nuts, my darling. You can't just get married in those countries. There are miles and miles of red tape." She wound her arms around his middle and laid her cheek on his chest. "It's a lovely idea though. Thank you for offering."

He threaded his hands into her hair and tilted her head back, his gaze skimming over her features with a hungry warmth. "You forget, my love. I have friends in high places. The president of the United States likes nothing better than to take his scissors to red tape."

FRANCE. The scent of grapes, heavy on the vines, and the warmth of the sun beaming down from a cloudless sky was a perfect *mise-en-scène* for a wedding, or so Miranda thought dreamily as she stood in the garden of the small inn in the shelter of her husband's arm. How in the world had they ever accomplished everything in only three days, she wondered.

She wore her grandmother's wedding gown, which had been carefully packed in her suitcase for the trans-Atlantic flight. Jake's morning coat was stretched to its limits across his broad shoulders. He'd borrowed it from Donald. The sunlight glinted in his dark hair, touched the planes of his face and shadowed his eyes as they met hers.

"How soon can we get away?" he growled in her ear.

She smiled and lifted her bouquet to inhale

the heady scent of white roses. "Five minutes?" she teased.

"Go and change your clothes. I'll bring the car around." They were driving south toward the Riviera, for their honeymoon. His warm gaze took in the members of the small wedding party, and he shook his head, grinning indulgently. "I don't believe they'll even miss us," he added.

The champagne had flowed freely, enough for several weddings. Taylor and her father had toasted each other over and over, as though they had arranged the whole thing themselves. Her mother sat on a wrought-iron bench in the shade, sipped from a crystal glass, and listened to Donald describe the events leading to this quite extraordinary occasion. Her tinkling laugh rang out frequently and Miranda wondered just what Donald was telling her.

"Jake?" She turned to him with an amused question in her green eyes.

He couldn't resist the temptation of her parted lips and covered them with a very tender kiss. "What, love?" he asked huskily.

"Doesn't it seem rather inappropriate that they are so happy to get us married off?"

His hand came up to cradle her face. "They probably took one look at the way I watch you and decided it was safer," he explained.

"Safer?" she asked blankly. He chuckled, and then she understood. "I suppose we'll be moving to Detroit pretty soon."

"Probably," he agreed, eyeing her with un-disguised relish.

She looked past his shoulder to the bench where her mother was sitting. Their gazes met, and her mother's eyelid dropped in a beguiling wink.

Miranda laughed with delight. Mary Louise Fitzgerald Woodbarry was going to make a very good grandmother.